PRAISE FOR *BRENNER AND GOD*

"A must for crime fiction lovers with a sense of humor: In Simon Brenner, Wolf Haas has created a protagonist so real and believable that I sometimes wanted to tap him on the shoulder and point him in the right direction!" **—ANDREY KURKOV, AUTHOR OF *DEATH AND THE PENGUIN***

"*Brenner and God* is one of the cleverest—and most thoroughly enjoyable—mysteries that I've read in a long time. Wolf Haas is the real deal, and his arrival on the American book scene is long overdue." **—CARL HIAASEN, AUTHOR OF *SICK PUPPY***

"A meticulously plotted, dark, and often very funny ride." **—THE MILLIONS**

"*Brenner and God* is a humdinger ... a sockdollager of an action yarn, revealed via the smart-ass, self-effacing narrative voice that's a sort of trademark of author Wolf Haas." **—THE AUSTIN CHRONICLE**

"[A] superb translation of one of Austria's finest crime novels ... Haas never loses the thread of investigation, even as he introduces off-beat characters and a very complex plot ... This is the first of the Brenner novels in English. We can only hope for more, soon." **—THE GLOBE AND MAIL (TORONTO)**

"Even as Haas darkens the mood of this sly and entertaining novel, he maintains its sardonically irreverent tone." **—THE BARNES & NOBLE REVIEW**

"A pacey and gripping read." **—EURO CRIME**

"A gleaming gem of a novel." **—CRIMESPREE MAGAZINE**

WOLF HAAS was born in 1960 in the Austrian province of Salzburg. He is the author of seven books in the bestselling Brenner mystery series, three of which have been adapted into major German-language films by director Wolfgang Murnberger. Among other prizes, the books in the series have been awarded the German Thriller Prize and the 2004 Literature Prize from the city of Vienna. Haas lives in Vienna.

ANNIE JANUSCH is the translator of the Art of the Novella series edition of Heinrich von Kleist's *The Duel*, as well as the first three books in Wolf Haas's Brenner series, *Brenner and God*, *The Bone Man*, and *Resurrection*.

COME, SWEET
DEATH!

WOLF HAAS

COME, SWEET DEATH!

TRANSLATED BY ANNIE JANUSCH

MELVILLE HOUSE
BROOKLYN · LONDON

MELVILLE
INTERNATIONAL
CRIME

MELVILLE INTERNATIONAL CRIME

COME, SWEET DEATH!

First published in Germany as *Komm, süßer Tod*

Copyright © 1998 by Rowohlt Taschenbuch Verlag GmbH,
Reinbeck bei Hamburg
Translation copyright © 2014 by Annie Janusch

First Melville House Printing: July 2014

The verses quoted from *St. Matthew's Passion*
are in Robert Bridges's 1899 translation.

Melville House Publishing   8 Blackstock Mews
145 Plymouth Street   and   Islington
Brooklyn, NY 11201   London N4 2BT

mhpbooks.com   facebook.com/mhpbooks   @melvillehouse

Library of Congress
Cataloging-in-Publication Data

Haas, Wolf.
   [*Komm, süsser Tod*. English]
   Come, sweet death! / Wolf Haas ; translated by Annie Janusch.
      pages   cm
   First published in Germany as *Komm, süsser Tod* 1998 by Rowohlt
Taschenbuch Verlag GmbH, Reinbeck bei Hamburg.
   ISBN 978-1-61219-339-7 (paperback)
   ISBN 978-1-61219-340-3 (ebook)
   1. Private investigators—Austria—Vienna—Fiction. 2. Ambulance
drivers—Austria—Vienna—Fiction. 3. Murder—Investigation—Aus-
tria—Vienna—Fiction. I. Janusch, Annie, translator. II. Title.

PT2708.A17K613 2014
833.92—dc23

                                              2014012225

Manufactured in the United States of America
1 3 5 7 9 10 8 6 4 2

The translation of this book was supported by the
Austrian Federal Ministry of Education, Arts, and Culture.

COME, SWEET DEATH!

CHAPTER 1

Well, something's happened again.

A day that starts off like this one can only get worse, though. Now I don't mean for that to sound somehow superstitious. I'm definitely not the type to get scared when a black cat crosses my path. Or an ambulance goes driving by, and you've got to make the sign of the cross right there on the spot—just so you won't be the next in line to get sliced up into a hundred thousand pieces by a CT scanner.

And Friday the Thirteenth, don't get me started. Because it was Monday the 23rd that Ettore Sulzenbacher was lying in the middle of Pötzleinsdorfer Strasse and crying so bad that it would've broke your heart.

When Frau Sulzenbacher found her son there, at first she thought he was just yammering on again about the name she'd given him some seven years ago. But then she saw the cause of his despair. Because there beside the bawling child was his dead cat, Ningnong.

An ambulance—lights flashing and sirens blaring—had squashed Ningnong. By the time Ettore discovered his dead black cat, though, the ambulance was already long gone. It'd gone barreling down Pötzleinsdorfer Strasse so fast that it was a stroke of luck that Ningnong had been the only victim.

And no amount of bawling on Ettore's part was going

to bring him back—the cat was gone. What I don't know is whether that's supposed to bring more bad luck or less when you run over a black cat that crosses your path.

Either way, Paramedic Manfred Big gave it zero thought at the time. He was en route at such a clip that he didn't even notice when his ambulance flattened Ningnong into a black omelette. He was in a hurry to catch the next red light.

Because when they're out on an emergency call nowadays, it's kind of trendy for ambulances to tally up how many intersections they can take against a red. A bit of a record-setting mentality, like you find everywhere today. The lawmakers have prohibited ambulances from proceeding through intersections against a red traffic signal. People just think it's allowed because they see it so often—an ambulance with lights and sirens, thundering through a red light. When in fact it's *verboten*. Red is red. Even for ambulances.

Even for Manfred Big, who his colleagues had always just called Bimbo. I don't know how he got that name, either, but I'd guess it had something to do with his bulging eyes and that thick red orangutan neck of his. And needless to say, the Jheri Curl wasn't exactly helping him any. But Bimbo was only twenty-eight and already starting to lose his hair a little, and a nurse, who'd been a hairstylist before she became a nurse, well, for 190 schillings, she gave him those glossy little curls and a private appointment, basically a cover-up. Interesting, though! The less hair he had on his head, the bigger and thicker his mustache seemed to get.

Now, red lights, *verboten*. Needless to say, Bimbo breezed right through the intersection. Because that was a way for the ambulance drivers to protest. Against the lawmakers.

There you are, risking your life for others, day in day out, just so you can scrape them off the street in the nick of time before the vultures do, but do you think you'd ever get a "Thank you" out of those tight-lipped lawmakers? Or that it'd kill them to let you blow a red light now and then? Forget it. The lawmakers just put obstacles in your path. And won't grant you a red. Purely legally speaking, of course.

Practically speaking, another thing altogether. Because Ningnong hadn't even landed splat on the asphalt yet before Bimbo Big was flitting through the next intersection against a red.

Because one thing you can't forget. Bimbo had this arrangement with a couple of his fellow EMTs. A little game. And why not, if it brings a little levity to the daily grind? An ambulance driver like that's got enough to put up with, and so I say, why shouldn't he be allowed a little fun, even if maybe—purely legally speaking—it doesn't quite obey the letter of the law?

Pay attention, this is how it works: When a dispatch came in over the radio, Bimbo would yell: "Five!" or "Eight!"—or, for all I care, "Three!"—for every location. And that meant how many minutes Bimbo thought he could make it in. And if his partner yelled back, "More!" then, that meant he accepted the bet. And if Bimbo's run took longer, his partner got a C-note, but if it didn't, he paid Bimbo the hundred.

But because Bimbo almost always made it, the EMTs were accepting his bets less and less. So Bimbo had to come up with times that were even more hair-raising to get them to take the bait. And then Bimbo would have to drive like the devil, of course.

I'm just saying: Südtirolerplatz to Taborstrasse, eight minutes, in rush hour, that's a suicide mission, and any EMT that rides along with him once is going to end up swearing to himself that he'll never bet against Bimbo again—not because the hundred bucks has him scared, mind you, but because he's scared he'll barely escape with his life.

Bimbo's partner on this day in question was Hansi Munz. A Monday—Hansi Munz would never forget it his whole life long. Not because Bimbo was tearing down the kilometer-long Gersthofer Strasse at the speed of hell, but because—hold on, though.

Bimbo wasn't daredeviling along, suicide-like, with lights and sirens, on account of some bet with Hansi Munz. Because Hansi Munz was such a tightwad that he never would've wagered even a schilling. But because Bimbo had to pick up a liver transplant from Vienna General.

"Milka!" Hansi Munz shouted all the sudden, as Bimbo pummeled down Wahringer Strasse at a hundred and twenty.

Because that was all he managed to get out when he saw the Milka chocolate truck parked outside the bank. Bimbo rushed the Milka truck without braking, though. And even though Hansi Munz knew just how sensitive Bimbo got when his co-driver acted more like a backseat driver, Hansi Munz just couldn't hold back any longer and out came a word of warning. Out of sheer fright, though, he didn't manage to blurt out more than just that one word, maybe because it's the kind of word you've known ever since you were a kid.

And believe it or not: Bimbo neither crashed into the Milka truck, nor did he swerve to the left at the very last second—and all the while, he did not brake.

No, with a big grin on his face he clattered to the right of the Milka truck—well, between the Milka truck and the bank—and up onto the sidewalk. And if an ambulance is two meters wide, then, between the Milka truck and the bank, there were maybe two hundred centimeters, definitely not a hair more than that. And Hansi Munz sure felt it—felt like the skin was getting grated off his shoulders a little, left and right, both, I'm talking flat-out bodily sympathy with the paint job.

But you've got to grant Bimbo this: he smuggled that ambulance between the Milka truck and the bank with real elegance, I don't know how he did it, but by the skin of his teeth somehow.

Hansi Munz, of course, huge sigh of relief. Because it wasn't just the damage to the paint job that made it seem like his goose bumps were flaking off. Even worse was the dread of what the boss would do to them if they came home with a dent.

"Junior's going to skin us alive if we bang up the new seven-forty."

"Nobody's banging up anything," Bimbo said, still smiling about his performance, as he bolted up the Währinger Gürtel in the wrong direction. Three lanes of one-way traffic were coming straight at them. They would've had the right of way on the other side of the beltway, but the hospital entrance—way too complicated.

"And what would you have done if the door to the Milka truck had swung open?"

"Ducked."

"You really are crazy."

"It's about the liver transplant, Munzi."

7

"If you keep on driving like that, it's only a matter of time before our organs are the ones getting donated. What would you have done if somebody had come out of the bank?"

"Nobody did."

"But if they had!"

"He would've been in luck. If you're going to get run over by a car these days, then you should count yourself lucky if it's an ambulance that does the running over. We would've put him right back on his feet."

"You've got a lot of nerve."

"Might as well retire if you don't have any nerve. Driving an ambulance is no kid's birthday party."

Hansi Munz could tell that Bimbo didn't want to hear anything else out of him right now, and in fact, Hansi Munz was glad, too, that they were still going to make it in time for the liver transplant.

Because it was three minutes before five, and they were practically there already. Thanks to the sidewalk action and going the wrong way on the one-way, Bimbo had definitely gained two minutes.

"Shit!" Bimbo yelled, as they approached the hospital entrance. Because from the opposite direction—swimming with the current, so to speak—the 720 was coming straight at them with lights and sirens.

"What kind of a jackass drives a seven-twenty today?"

Needless to say, the 720 wasn't going to yield a millimeter. All of ten meters from their front bumper, it shot into the main gate.

"Lanz."

"Of all people."

Bimbo didn't want to believe that an old ninny like Lanz had outdone him on a liver run.

"We can still make it," Hansi Munz said, trying to calm Bimbo down.

The vehicle hadn't even come to a complete stop before Bimbo was already out the door. Because on odd days, it was the driver who always did the liver runs, and on even days his partner did—that was the ancient agreement between Bimbo and Hansi Munz. And today, Monday the 23rd, odd day, Hansi Munz would never forget it, even if he lived to be a hundred and ten years old like Frau Süssenbrunner, who they'd driven to her Parkinson's therapy for the last time just two weeks ago.

It was maybe fifteen, twenty meters from where they were parked over to Rosi's. Because her stand was on the lawn, right next to the new music pavilion. Still more than a minute left to cover those fifteen meters, Bimbo really didn't have to run like that. Two liver transplants with pepperoni and sweet mustard—they'd still get their orders in before it closed at five. Because Rosi was strict about that: whoever orders before five gets something, but when the clock strikes five, she doesn't take any more orders.

Hansi Munz's stomach was already growling, and he was annoyed now, too, that Bimbo had to get in line behind Lanz. He had prepared himself for the eventuality that it could be a little while before he got his hot liver transplant. I don't know, either—the expression got started at some point by one of the EMTs, and now all of them use it. Then, a few years ago, even Rosi herself started writing it on the chalkboard next to the pickup window: *liver transplant 32, heart transplant* 60 (that was back then, today it's already up to 39 schillings for a liver transplant, and just you wait, only a matter of time before the forty-schilling sound barrier gets broken, too).

Needless to say, though, complaints from patients, and the hospital lawyer got to be a little too much for Rosi, so, obligingly, she went back to writing on her chalkboard: ¼ *kilo Leberkäse* and ½ *kilo Leberkäse*. But the lawyer can't do a thing, of course, about how people talk, so it'll be a liver transplant for the lesser appetite and a heart transplant for the hardier eaters from now until the end of time.

And after all that excitement, Hansi Munz had worked up such an appetite that he was almost sorry he'd only asked Bimbo to order him a liver transplant. On the other hand, there was no way anyone could be hungry enough to finish off a heart transplant without getting sick.

He may have been hungry, but Hansi Munz wasn't bored. There, in the narrow pathway between Rosi's stand and the music pavilion, was a pair of lovers in need of no Leberkäse at all. Because the real danger was that the two of them would devour each other.

The woman had on a white lab coat, and she was at least a head shorter than the man who was cramming his head into her neck—just watching was enough to make Hansi Munz's neck sore.

"That dirty bitch," Hansi Munz muttered as the nurse tilted her neck back even farther.

He was in no hurry for Bimbo to come back now because, at least this way, he could enjoy their performance in peace.

"What a dirty bitch," he said aloud, over and over again, even though he wasn't quite at the age where a person's apt to soliloquize. Hansi Munz was just a drop over thirty, although people always thought he was older on account of his stodgy ways. And needless to say, his old-fashioned glasses and his thinning hair didn't do much, either, to make him look any younger. And even the faintly pubescent down on his upper lip didn't make him look youthful—no, just stunted.

But today, might as well be spring for Hansi. "Irmi, you dirty bitch." Suddenly he was on a first-name-basis with the nurse—and sitting not fifteen meters away in a vehicle with the doors closed and watching her through the windshield.

He was panting as though Irmi was as close to him as the tall pale man in the dark-gray suit was to her. There, between Rosi's stand and the music pavilion, the man was giving that nurse such a working-over that you'd have thought: That's no kiss, it's a tonsillectomy, and all the operating rooms in Ear, Nose & Throat must be booked full-up.

Hansi Munz was getting so hot watching the nurse slide slowly down her lover's chest, one centimeter at a time, that the windshield was getting fogged up now.

"What're you doing now?" Hansi Munz asked the dirty bitch from behind the windshield.

Seconds later, he was out the car door—even faster than Bimbo. But not because he couldn't stand the excitement anymore. Aw, I don't want to make Hansi Munz out to be any worse than he already is. Okay, excitement maybe, sure, but not like that, no. Excitement insofar as a person's apt to get excited when he sees what a medic like Munz saw right then and there.

Because the nurse just kept sliding. And then, the man slid down after her, too. And the two of them kept on sliding down. Until they were lying on the strip of grass between Rosi's stand and the music pavilion, completely motionless.

That got Munz so excited that he practically tore the car door off its Mercedes hinges and stormed right over to the two of them.

By then, though, all he could determine was that they were dead. Well, officially an EMT can't do that. Because only doctors can do that. But to be out of luck the way this nurse was out of luck, you just have to see for yourself. The man in the dark gray suit had been shot so savagely that the bullet exited into the nurse.

From the make-out king's neck, the bullet didn't have very far to go to get to his mouth. And needless to say, both their mouths, wide open, so the bullet just kept on traveling, just like that, right into the nurse's brain.

So you see, this is what I was trying to say before. The reason why Hansi Munz wouldn't forget the date any time soon. Monday, May 23, 5:03 p.m.

CHAPTER 2

When you work for the EMS in this day and age, you've got yourself the kind of profession where you can say: *People respect me for it.* Not so much for a nightclub owner, where morally it's not quite, you know, or a car dealer, where maybe people say: No amount of snake oil could keep that bucket from rusting. Saving lives, though, people say: a sweet business.

And Brenner, he knew the flip side of that, too. Because, after all, he'd been on the police force for almost twenty years, and you'd like to think a police officer would deserve a certain amount of respect, too, for paying his dues to society and whatnot. But, no, society is often a little unfair to police officers. Society goes around giving cops nicknames that essentially can't be used in the same sentence as the word "respect." I don't know where that comes from, maybe out of some fear that cops could just go around arresting all of society. As if saying a friendly word to a pig is going to somehow tip the balance, and voilà, police state. But that's not the reason why, after nineteen years on the force, Brenner threw it all away. Just between us: I don't think he himself knew why, exactly. Because he was forty-four at the time, and it goes without saying, that's an age where a man's prone to doing something a little impulsive.

Then, he worked as a detective for a little while, and so, all that talk about respect, completely out the window, of course. In fact, it made him realize that his standing as a cop hadn't been all that bad. Police, maybe not ideal, but detective, no way. And some days he didn't dare say how he earned his money—dirty laundry, so to speak.

Needless to say, he told his former colleague Fadinger, who he ran into six months ago at the train station here in Vienna. And Fadinger was the one who'd told Brenner about how he'd made the switch ten years ago from being a cop to working blood-donor services. Because, a cushy job, and the overtime's better than with the police. And when Fadinger mentioned that they were looking for a driver just then over at Vienna Rapid Response, Brenner was interested right away. He didn't have anything against moving to Vienna, either. Because since he'd quit the police, he didn't really know anymore where home was anyway.

For as long as he was on the force, he'd had his civil service apartment, cheap rent and all. But when, two and a half years ago, he went off the force, well, apartment gone, too, of course. And he'd been gypsying around ever since—a little murder here, lodging thrown in gratis, a little embezzlement there, a room at the company hotel.

I don't mean to say that he was particularly bothered by the situation. Quite the opposite, it even had its advantages. Of course, his position with the EMS had its advantages, too—namely, a seventy-square-meter apartment.

In that sense, the Vienna Rapid Response was wonderfully designed. A spacious inner courtyard that thirty garage bays opened out onto, plus a vehicle-repair workshop and a crew room. And in the middle of the courtyard, a magnificent glass pavilion, which was the dispatch center. And above the garages, living quarters for the EMTs. So that in your free time you could look down at the courtyard and watch your colleagues having to work.

I suspect the main reason why Brenner even took the job was the apartment. And not the prestige. Because these days, when you're forty-seven years old and lacking considerable standing, then, as we say in German: You don't give a damn about the years you've got left, either.

Although Brenner was still a kid back when people used to say that. Don't just think about retirement—not just mortgage and life insurance—but the meaningful stuff, too, a little. Yeah, today you laugh about it, but back then, it was the latest thing. You've got to picture it like this: like how today we've got roller skates, or better yet, a mountain bike. Well, people used to have their things, too.

And maybe the fact that Brenner himself got rescued by the EMS just last year played some small part, too. That was when his pinky finger got hacked off—it was even big in the newspapers. Got sewed back on, thank god—nearly bled to death, though. Hopped out of the gravedigger's shovel right at the last second.

Just so you understand why all the sudden Brenner's sitting in an EMT uniform in the crew room. He was leafing through an issue of *Bunte*, because it was one of those godawful days where absolutely nothing was going on. In all of Vienna, apparently, no heart attack, no accident, no suicide, no nothing. And the teenage suicide season wasn't officially underway yet, either, because it'd be another five weeks before any diplomas got handed out.

And the Danube Island Festival wouldn't be for a few

weeks yet, either. Where you end up having to admit half of Vienna—that's almost a million people with alcohol poisoning. The Office of Cultural Affairs thought about just draining the whole Danube for the sake of the festival and filling it with free beer, so they could spare themselves having to set up all those booths, and just drive people to the river banks instead, but unfortunately, the technology's not there yet.

Today, though, no trace of any of that kind of fun. And a day like this at Vienna Rapid Response was cause for despair: ten, twenty grown men sitting around the crew room, bored to death.

"Well, that's a coincidence," EMT Marksteiner muttered, pointing at the page in *Bunte* that Brenner was reading just now. Brenner acted like he didn't notice that Marksteiner was talking to him, but for Marksteiner, that was just a reason to double his volume: "Look at the clock, Brenner!"

"You don't know what time it is?" As Brenner said this, though, he was already looking up at the clock on the wall, a white kitchen clock with black hands, that had definitely been put through its thirty years. Somebody must've gone to some effort to hang the old kitchen clock, whose hands were now pointing right at the twelve, here in the new, supermodern Rapid Response Center.

"High noon!" Marksteiner said triumphantly.

"So?"

"So, you're reading an article about Stephanie of Monaco."

"So?"

"And her mom was in the old western *High Noon!*"

Because when you're sitting around the crew room like this and waiting for an emergency, it's only a matter of time before a coincidence is good enough for staving off the boredom a little.

"Female lead," Lil' Berti said, butting into the conversation now. He was six foot three and thin as a pencil, but his whole life long, nickname, Lil' Berti.

"Like she would've played the male lead, c'mon!" Marksteiner said, and with that, the conversation ended just as fast as he'd instigated it. Because Lil' Berti was just an 8K. Thanks to the government's Volunteers in Service to Austria Act, i.e. Public Law 8000. And a career medic can't very well let some 8K interrupt him.

VISTAA was also the reason why Lil' Berti sometimes got on Brenner's nerves a little. Even though he was definitely one of the nicer ones. Somebody who even got in the vehicle sometimes, get this—with no sunglasses on. But he was unhappy in his job and ever since he'd heard that Brenner used to be a detective, he'd fallen in love with the idea of opening up a detective agency with Brenner.

And today was exactly the kind of day when there was a real danger of him starting in on it again. Because time just wasn't passing. At a quarter after twelve, still no emergency. And at twelve-thirty, still no emergency.

For the third time already today, Bimbo took his gold chain from around his red, gym-rat's neck and poked the dirt out from between the individual links with his fingernails. "Crazy how fast these twist links get dirty!" Bimbo yelled, and about as irritably as if he had to teach one of the volunteers how to wash the ambulances.

But it was just his gold chain that he was cursing at. They did away with most of the volunteers two years ago. Since then, any advantage they'd had over Pro Med Vienna had been eroded. Nevertheless, Bimbo was glad that he didn't have to see any more of those wimps.

"I wonder where all this grime comes from!" Bimbo said, cursing his gold chain. "Can you imagine, all this dirt's just in the air! And we're breathing this dirt in all the time!"

"Maybe it's not in the air at all," Lil' Berti said, this time butting into the conversation between Bimbo and his gold chain.

When the government canceled all the volunteer programs, a few 8Ks got kept on staff. It goes without saying, though, the 8Ks would always remain interns more or less. And so, once again, Lil' Berti's nickname was an advantage, because the other five didn't have names at all, just the collective name "8K."

The redness of Bimbo's neck was rising to his head now, as if Berti had called him god knows what. Because one thing you can't forget. Bimbo had been sitting in the crew room for an hour and a half already. One and a half hours of no red lights. Not even a shitty assignment like a *Scheisshäusltour*. And so, certain aggressions start stockpiling.

"What did you say, you little twerp?" Bimbo yelled, even though he was, at most, five years older than Lil' Berti. "Where else would it come from, then? You think the gold in the chain causes it?"

"Or maybe your neck does."

Here we go. The damn thing was that everybody else laughed. And Bimbo knew for a fact: fighting on duty, strictly *verboten*. So, he slowly places the gold chain back around his neck. And then he says: "I wouldn't even lay a finger on an Eight-K like you."

It was quiet for the next five minutes, so Brenner was able to study the sex scandals in the British royal family in peace and quiet. But then, Marksteiner again: "I've always said, it's all the horseback riding they do—those blue-bloods getting off on it."

Marksteiner had this impossible habit. He never would've picked a magazine up off the pile himself, even if he had to sit all day long in the crew room. But no sooner would another person start reading an article than he'd be adding his dose of mustard to it.

At quarter to one, Brenner put his issue of *Bunte* back on the pile, and when he looked up at the kitchen clock ten minutes later, it was still quarter to one. But don't go thinking the kitchen clock had stopped. Because the cleaning lady set it every morning, so that wasn't it. Just Brenner's inner clock that was on the fritz due to boredom.

And finally, at one, still no emergency. "That's the crazy thing about our job," Bimbo said, breaking his own silence. "Because we're always outside in the filthy air, always out in the middle of traffic. I can see it on my gold chain. But you know what, I'll tell you. My new one that I had on yesterday doesn't get dirty at all. It doesn't soak up the dirt!"

Because just last week Bimbo had bought himself a new gold chain that was three times as expensive as his most expensive old one. The thinnest and yet the most expensive! And today was the first day where, just to switch things up, he was wearing one of the old ones. To compensate, though, he had to at least talk about the new one: "Because it's only the Figaro chains that get filthy! But my new one ain't a Figaro! It's hand-riveted! You can hang a five-hundred-kilo weight from it, and it won't break! And dirt don't stick to it, either!"

"What do you still wear the old junk for, then?" That was old Lanz intervening just now—you know, Lanz, who'd beat him to Rosi's two weeks ago.

And Bimbo, red like a stop light all over again: "What're you calling old junk? You think I'm going to go and throw all the others away now? Just because they're Figaros. No, I'm always changing 'em up. Just like with the ladies."

Old Lanz immediately fell silent. Because needless to say, Bimbo and Lanz's daughter. That'd been the talk of the station for a few days now.

"Yeah, yeah. Not every day's Sunday," Hansi Munz chimed in, but more half asleep. "One day there's so much going on that you can barely keep up with the work, and before you can clean up all the suicide brains off the vacuum mattress, you're already packing up for a heart attack."

"When do you clean the vacuum mattress, then?"

"And then"—Hansi Munz wasn't going to let himself get interrupted by Bimbo—"even the *Scheisshäusltouren* get going."

Now, to explain: The exciting calls are always in the minority. It's the *Scheisshäusltouren* that usually make up your day: delivering a granny to dialysis and picking her back up again two hours later. Delivering a patient from Wilhelminen Hospital to the Brothers of Mercy, and then, while you're there, picking up another patient from the Brothers of Mercy and delivering that one to Vienna General. Or a cooler of donated blood from the blood donation center to the trauma center. Or Parkinson's therapy. Or eldercise. Because there are people whose health coverage includes all sorts of things, and with them, you've just got to be thankful that you're not driving them to the coffee shop.

The bell went off much less often than the chime that the dispatch center used to signal the routine calls. Routine calls, thank you. I don't always want to be saying *Scheiss-häusltouren*, it's not a very nice word. And it's only with emergencies that the dispatch center sounds that shrill buzz of a bell—and if Junior catches you and you're not up and out the door, there's a hailstorm, don't even ask.

Junior took the business over from his father five years ago, and even though he himself wasn't exactly the youngest anymore, everybody still called him Junior. But if he caught you loafing, then, make no mistake, you knew who the boss was around here.

A hailstorm from Junior still would've been preferable to all this miserable waiting around for some sweaty manager's heart to stop ticking somewhere in some part of the city. But nothing doing. Today, neither bell nor chime. Today, just Stephanie of Monaco and Buckingham Palace. Brenner was already on his third issue of *Bunte*, and this whole time, the chime and the bell didn't go off once.

But the intercom did: "Herr Brenner, please report to the dispatch center."

Officially, they had to be quite formal, especially over the radio, because international radio rules and all. And intercom, needless to say, a little bit like radio.

Generally, you weren't too happy to get summoned to the dispatch center. Because your colleagues in the dispatch center are a little, how should I put it: more militant than the military.

But today, Brenner was just glad for the change of pace. When that fat Nuttinger saw him on the surveillance screen, he met him right at the door, and then Brenner was already getting an earful: "Brenner! Change in drivers! Junior needs Herr Big to drive."

Because, officially, Bimbo was still called Big, and to-day, Brenner was supposed to drive with Bimbo—every day a different duo, according to the principle of rotation. And switching up drivers, that was a reform that Junior had introduced. Junior sure doted on Bimbo, though. And the sparrows were already chirping from the rooftops that Bimbo was next in line for a promotion.

"You're to leave immediately. Take the seven-seventy. Schimpl's driving," fat Nuttinger commanded, and then all of the sudden in a very different tone of voice: "Vienna Rapid Response Center?"

Because that was meant for the orange emergency phone. And a second later, fat Nuttinger was pressing the bell. And a second after that, he was barking in Brenner's face from half a centimeter away: "Hop to it, Brenner! On the double!"

And Brenner was only just now grasping that, because of the change in drivers, he'd just slipped up the rotation wheel from the seventh slot all the way up to the first slot, and that meant he had to take this emergency call with his new partner.

Schimpl was already waiting in the vehicle when Brenner

finally came running out. Brenner was already apprehensive that Schimpl would start lecturing him right away, because he was one of those people who give their unsolicited opinions to all and sundry. And then, as a matter of fact, a lecture, but not about Brenner's dawdling.

Because "Franz Josef Station. Fifteen S." was coming in over the radio now. And so Schimpl felt compelled to explain the underlying problem to Brenner: "It's insane how many sandlers we've got in this city. It's getting to be practically every other call now. Get this, we're allowed to play taxi to Herr Sandler, but we're not even allowed to say sandler anymore. No, these days, you've got to say *homeless*."

You should know, 15 S was the radio code for an unconscious sandler. That was the only radio code with an S, otherwise just numbers, because where in the world have you seen a radio code with an S in it. But 15's unconsciousness, and S is just a covert way to indicate a sandler.

Of course, indicating something like that's *verboten*—only information about the type of emergency, not the type of person. Strictly insofar as humanitarian things go internationally, it's not in compliance. On the other hand, it actually does provide the driver with a certain amount of orientation when he gets the S. Because for every code 15 you get, you're risking life and limb for an unconscious person. And then, when you get there and it's just a drunk sandler, well, as an EMT, you've got to watch out that you don't cause him a little 15 with your own shoe.

Maybe that sounds brutal, but you can't forget the hormones that come pouring out of you when you're driving in full-on lights-and-sirens emergency mode. Starting with adrenaline all the way to—but I'm no doctor. All I know's that these hormones make you aggressive. Because you actually need the aggression if you're going to be charging through a couple of red lights and shooing cars and bicycles and pedestrians over to the side everywhere you go.

And then, when you meet a drunk Sandler, who you've put your life on the line for, needless to say, your vaccine wears off a little.

That's why Junior decided at some point, We'd better add the S. You drive more leisurely when it's a sandler, and that way, you don't get as aggressive. I think it was five, six years back now that there was that sandler story about the head injury. You know, where the newspapers wrote about it.

The drunk fell onto the sidewalk, and then, so it said in the newspapers, he got a little, well, by the EMT—clumsily handled, i.e. intent. Personally, I can't fathom it, and you can't believe everything that's in the papers today.

But Junior, of course, always thinking about the public. And it's better that way, too, because without donors, you might as well pack it in. Blood donors, organ donors, money donors, all of them. Now, he invented the code S for the radio. And I've got to say, great invention. A hundred years from now, we might not know anything else about Junior except that he invented the code S. Because ever since he did, the EMTs? Much less aggressive when they have to go on a sandler call.

That's why Schimpl was already jabbering on about it on the drive over now, because, from the S, he knew exactly who they'd be meeting there. "I'll tell you something: you give a homeless guy a home, and he'll be burning that house down before the day is done. And you know why? Because he can't stand being under a roof. So nobody better come to me and start talking about the poor homeless. Because we used to call them sandlers. And it's still a better word for them if you ask me. Because a sandler wants to sleep in the sand. A home, though, he doesn't really want one. So why shouldn't I say sandler?"

"Go right ahead and say it."

"And I will."

Brenner hoped that he'd momentarily cut off the power to his cranky commentary. But not with Schimpl:

"And another thing. Because, it's getting to the point these days that a person can't say what he thinks anymore."

"You always do."

"I always do." Schimpl took it as a compliment—and as license to keep on talking with all-new zeal. He explained to Brenner that there are different types of sandlers. As if Brenner didn't know that already. As if Brenner didn't have to pick up a couple of sandlers off the streets every single day. Schimpl, though, was very precise in his classifications of them, like a butterfly collector. All according to cause: bad family, bad divorce, bad character, bad accident.

So you can imagine that Brenner was pretty happy when he saw Franz Josef Station up ahead. In spite of the code S, at the last intersection, he ran the red light out of sheer relief. Like those confused drivers who seem to fall asleep at the wheel when the light goes to green, and only accelerate as it's turning red.

"S!" Schimpl yelled, frantic, because he'd compartmentalized his life so rationally that he couldn't comprehend whatsoever why Brenner would risk chauffeuring them under a truck. And then, needless to say, brain contusions, and then, loss of inhibitions, and then, sex maniac, and then, found guilty, divorced, and then: sandler. We've seen it all before!

But thank god there was no more time to discuss it now.

Because the station master was already motioning to them. An old railway man with teeth like that French actor. Usually I can't stand French movies, the way, oftentimes, nothing gets said for ten minutes. But this one was good, with the guy who always played Don Camillo, and when he laughed: teeth like a horse.

The station master wasn't laughing, though. Surprised, he asked: "What're you two doing here?"

"We got called by the luggage office. You've got another sandler in the storage lockers."

"Wasn't the luggage office that called. I called it in myself—fifteen minutes ago! It's been happening almost every day now that those little shits go and shut some sandler up in a locker."

"Shut them in! Don't make me laugh," Schimpl protested. "They shut themselves up in there. To them, it's a cheap place to sleep."

"Maybe, but they don't *lock* themselves in," the railway man said, cutting Schimpl short.

"In some countries, they don't even have lockers anymore, on account of the bomb threats." Schimpl always knew better. "And soon there won't be any more here, either, because every locker's getting converted into a hotel room for Herr Homeless."

Now, this was just starting to get uncomfortable for Brenner, and he said to the railway man with the Don Camillo teeth: "It's worth the twenty schillings to those little shits that some poor schmuck spends a few hours scared to death."

"Most of the time, one of my men hears them banging and lets them right back out. Then, it's not so bad. But this one today was half dead. Shit himself right up to his neck out of fright."

"Cry me a river," Schimpl chimed back in. "Where is he, then?"

"Well, that's why I'm surprised."

And then the station master gave Brenner a look of slight embarrassment. The railway man with the horse face suddenly got about as taciturn as a French film.

"What do you mean, 'surprised'?" Schimpl wanted to know.

"Well, I'm surprised you're still here. Pro Med Vienna already came and took him away five minutes ago."

"What do you mean, 'Pro Med Vienna'?"

"Just what I said, Pro Med Vienna."

"Did you call them, too, or something?"

"What did I tell you?"

"What do you mean, what did you tell me?"

You see, that's why I've always said: Court interpreter, or maybe professor, those would've been the right careers for Schimpl. EMT, though, he was just too easily ruffled.

Especially now. When the old railway man said: "I was surprised, too, that they came. And just five minutes before you did, no less."

And to tell you the truth, Brenner was getting a little ruffled now, too. Because one thing you can't forget. For a Rapid Responder, there's nothing worse than when a call gets snatched right out from under your nose by your EMS rival, Pro Med.

CHAPTER 3

By the end of his shift, Brenner had completely forgot about the incident at Franz Josef Station. He couldn't have known just how often in the coming days he'd find himself still thinking about that snatched-up sandler. Maybe it was a premonition somehow that he was sitting in his apartment as cranky as he was this evening.

He watched TV till nine, and then he began deliberations. I don't mean to say: melancholic, just a little, you know, like how his grandmother always used to say to him, very stern: "This is why you shouldn't brood!"

Now, too, as he sat in his apartment, he could've used someone to give him a shake and remind him: "You shouldn't brood!"

But with honest-to-goodness brooding, you don't typically brood over something concrete. Brooding for the sake of brooding, as it were. Tonight, though, Brenner was brooding over whether he should still go down to the Kellerstüberl for a beer or not.

It goes without saying, though, when you've been brooding over a dilemma like this for three hours, you're pretty close to certified brooding. He could see from his apartment that the lights were still on in the bar down in the basement below the crew room. Every night there were poker games down there, and his co-workers often played for money, don't even ask. The element of risk from working in emergency services gets so ingrained that, even after your shift ends, you still need it.

But instead of going down to the Kellerstüberl, he brooded his way back to the first time he'd ever been in a Kellerstüberl. Because one thing you can't forget: When Brenner was a kid, the War still wasn't all that long ago. People were just glad to have a roof over their heads. Then came the years when people were putting in new heating systems. And then, the years when everybody was getting a new bathroom installed. And then, the years when everybody was getting new furniture. And then, the years when everybody was getting a new kitchen put in. And then came the years when everybody had everything.

And then came the year—I remember it exactly, 1968, when the Olympic Games were in Grenoble—when everybody was building a bar in their basement, what we call a Kellerstüberl.

Back then, Brenner would give his grandfather a hand in his carpentry workshop during school vacations. And on this particular vacation, they had to dress up the ceilings of ten Kellerstüberls with wood paneling. Every Kellerstüberl had its own character somehow, and somehow every Kellerstüberl was exactly the same. An overstuffed L-shaped sectional, a black coffee table. A fold-out bar with interior lights, full of cheap whisky and cognac. A lit-up Venetian gondola. A turntable with three Elvis records, or, for my part, "Take the A-Train." And a wood-paneled ceiling with recessed lighting.

And Brenner, needless to say, of a certain age at the time. Because in the winter of 1968, Brenner was, hold on, a good seventeen years old. All I'll say is this: wood paneling wasn't the only thing he nailed in the various Kellerstüberls of his summer vacation. Girls, too, so to speak. But enough about that. What it comes down to is this: You shouldn't brood!

At midnight Brenner finally realized this, too. But a bad sign must've been hanging over him today. Because instead of just going to sleep and putting an end to his bad day, he went down to the Kellerstüberl anyway.

When he first started working here, he'd often pop down for a beer. But ever since Bimbo and Munz made it into the *Kronenzeitung*, things had got a little trying with his co-workers. I don't mean to say megalomania, but, well, get a load of this.

Surely you're familiar with how the newspapers are always taking these photos where people are pointing off in some direction. Let's say somebody rescues a kid out of some raging torrent of a river. Then, some press photographer goes and says to the brave mensch: Stand over there and point at the river. And beneath the photo it says: "The brave child rescuer points to the treacherous rapids from which he rescued the child." Or somebody sees a UFO, and he points to the place where he saw the UFO. Or somebody breaks into your house, and you point to the empty place where, until recently, your entertainment center once stood.

No other examples are coming to me now, but I think you get the general idea. And that's exactly how Bimbo and Hansi Munz were pointing at Rosi's stand outside Vienna General in the newspaper, where the director of the Vienna blood bank was so savagely shot that it took his girlfriend Irmi right with him.

"AMBULANCE ARRIVES WITHIN SECONDS—TOO LATE" was the headline. And beneath the photo it said: "First Responders Big and Munz point to the place where Leo Stenzl and his paramour were struck down."

When you read something like that in the newspaper, you might well be troubled by the kinds of things that go on in the world. But you don't think about what a photo like that can do to a person like Bimbo.

Bimbo immediately exchanged his Ray-Bans for a pair of mirrored sunglasses: "So that my groupies out on the streets don't rip me right out of my vehicle," he was constantly saying. Or: "So that those lusty nurses over at the trauma center don't start nibbling at me before they've even stuffed their patients into the elevator." Doesn't matter, though, what Bimbo said—ever since his photo appeared in the *Kronenzeitung*, he just said it twice as loud as he used to. And he never used to be the quietest, either.

You're going to say, Maybe Brenner was just jealous of Bimbo's fame. But I've got to tell you, save the psychologizing for somebody else.

When, shortly before midnight, Brenner opened the door to the Kellerstüberl, he was almost sorry that he'd left his apartment. Because the curtain of haze that met him, that was no joke. Unbelievable how six, seven EMTs could produce a haze like that.

The haze wasn't just from the cigarettes, though. Although it was about as smoky as a high school bathroom in there. And it wasn't just the beer haze, either, even though all three tables were overflowing with empty and half-full beer bottles. The Kellerstüberl was just way too small for the Rapid Response Center. Two average-sized rounds of poker, and it was already crowded. And when you've got six men in there, smoking for hours on end, and seven men drinking—because Hansi Munz didn't smoke—you'd like to think that's reason enough for there to be a haze.

And it would've been enough, too—it would've been three times enough. But that wasn't even all of it.

You see, we didn't used to know this, but today we do. About the hormones. The sexual ones. There's a hormone all its own for that—that nature gave us, I mean—and there's nothing inherently bad about it, either. And the men have got their own and the women have got their own.

The men's one is called testosterone, technical term, as it were, but the EMTs know their way around technical terms a little. Because, courses and training, the works. But you don't actually have to know your way around technical terms—anybody that set foot in the Kellerstüberl at that moment would've had to struggle to keep from passing out. Because the air was practically held together by testosterone.

Back to the science again: when the man is sexually en route, so to speak, his body just pumps out this hormone. And when you've got seven men en route—because Hansi Munz, although he didn't smoke, testosterone nonetheless— and it's just a small room, like it was in the Kellerstüberl, then—that's a smell I don't want to describe in any detail.

Now, Why the smell? you're asking yourself.

I said: six men were smoking and one was not. But I haven't even got to the feminine side yet. Because there was also a woman there. Old Lanz's daughter, sitting right in the thick of all these EMTs, and you could tell right away that she already had a few beers in her.

Angelika still lived with her father, even though she was fast approaching twenty-five. But her mother died when she was sixteen, and ever since then, she's run the household a bit for her father.

But don't go thinking Angelika was a child of grief. Quite the opposite. Because she was the only young, unmarried woman living at the Rapid Response Center. And surrounded by any number of men, young and athletic and in uniform and everything. Needless to say, Angelika got a little curious, too, now and then, about what's under that uniform.

But that's how people are. You appreciate what's off in the distance more than you do what's under your nose. Now, over the past few years, Angelika had sampled her way through the ranks of the Vienna Rapid Response a bit, but it was only six months ago that she truly fell in love—with the boss of Pro Med Vienna of all people!

Needless to say, major hullabaloo among the Rapid Responders, but before the rumor ever really got off the ground, it was already over between Angelika and the Pro Meddler, and at least that way, she didn't have to move out of the Rapid Response Center.

For a few months there, Angelika had been looking as if god knows what kind of fish had slipped through her fingers, but a few days ago, she was seen talking to Bimbo for an hour and a half down in the courtyard, and now here she is, first time back down in the Kellerstüberl again.

Her hair, bleached and ruined by some beauty-shop butcher, seemed to have awoken to new life—I don't know if it was due to the witching hour or the recessed lighting or the hormones or Bimbo, who happened to be giving her a light with his Zippo just now.

"Suck!" Bimbo roared at Daughter Lanz, as he held a humongous flame to her that nearly sent Angelika's straw-dry mane up in flames. "Suck! Don't blow, Angelika!"

But Angelika Lanz already knew that when it comes to cigarettes, you've got to inhale, because she'd chain-smoked her way through the last ten years. And what Bimbo explained to her next, she'd also already heard hundreds of times:

"That's why they're called suckerettes." This was Bimbo, mind you. Anyway, she played along, inhaling a deep lungful so that the tip of the cigarette glowed orange like a Roman candle.

"Suck! Don't blow, Angelika," Bimbo said again, but provocatively quiet for how drunk he was now.

"Sure," Angelika answered softly and poured a little beer into her half-empty glass.

"What do you mean, 'sure'?" Bimbo asked. "Are you gonna give me a cigarette, too?"

"Sure." Angelika held out her pack of Kims to him. Bimbo took a good look around, smirking, as he took one of her chick-cigarettes. Then he placed his Zippo on the coffee table in front of Angelika: "Do you have a light?"

"Sure." Angelika took the lighter carefully in her hand, so as not to break off one of her five-centimeter-long nails, and gave Bimbo a light with his own lighter. "Suck, don't blow, Bimbo," Angelika said.

"Don't blow?" Bimbo asked.

Now, of course. One word begets the other.

And alcohol involved. Its disinhibiting effect's well documented. Although you're often sorry the next day and would like not to be reminded of it.

But Brenner sure remembered every detail the next morning. How Angelika took Bimbo at his word, right then and there before his assembled crew. How she made Bimbo glow like the orange tip of a cigarette in front of her father's raucous co-workers, who cheered her on like she was a striker in the Bundesliga.

What I don't know is if Angelika still remembered it all the next morning, or if she was sorry. After all, she lived in the same place as the very men who, for five whole minutes, transformed the Kellerstüberl into a hornet's nest.

All I know is this: Bimbo sure as hell wasn't sorry, because he was the big hero the next day. He sat in the crew room, happy as a pig in muck, rehashing his escapades from the night before with a few co-workers.

When old Lanz came in, at first they all fell silent. But then, Lanz lit a cigarette.

And then, needless to say, Bimbo: "Suck! Don't blow, old man!"

And then, the others completely lost it. You'd have thought the entire incident had been suppressed for millennia only to bust forth here and now in the presence of this handful of EMTs. That's how amusing Bimbo's remark was.

Old Lanz's face was burning, almost as red as Bimbo's the night before, when Angelika had taught him how to smoke.

And as Hansi Munz and the others proceeded to make ever more explicit insinuations as to what kind of a masterpiece Daughter Lanz had performed on Bimbo while completely drunk the night before, Lanz simply walked out and finished his cigarette in the courtyard. Before old Lanz was safely out of earshot, though, Munz quickly crunched the numbers for Bimbo: "For that, you would've had to shell out at least three thousand schillings with a professional."

"At least," Bimbo crowed. "And even then—nowhere near as good as with Lanzette."

Now, Brenner had been on the police force for nineteen years. And needless to say, you experience things along these same lines there, too. I don't want to sugarcoat anything now. You know that old chestnut, "Call the cops! A woman's been raped—oops, too late, they're already here." Well, it often checked out.

Or maybe it wasn't a chestnut so much as a jestnut that the police would sometimes say in and among their own ranks. And I don't even know if they still say it today now that all the nice old adages have wound up forgotten. That's just the natural course of things, though, you can't be old-fashioned and accentuating the negative all the time.

But every jestnut contains a kernel of seriousness. And there've been a few cases already that I'd rather not speak of. For your protection more than mine. And yet, you've got to admit: compared to the EMTs, Brenner's colleagues on the force were real mensches.

But Brenner didn't have much time to give this any thought now. The bell went off, and he was up and hoofing it past Lanz, who was just putting his cigarette out on

the windowsill. And from that alone you could tell that old
Lanz really wasn't doing too well. Because, for whatever rea-
son, the windowsills in the courtyard were sacred to Junior.
And if he had seen that, don't even ask.

As he ran, Brenner noticed that he was still feeling last
night's Kellerstüberl antics. But, old saying, nothing to do
but bite on through! Join the fun, i.e. join the 770. And
watch out that you don't puke in your own vehicle. Start the
engine, shift into drive, two-way radio:

"Seven-seventy headed out."

"Seven-seventy copy. Proceed with lights and sirens to
Per-Albin-Hansson-Siedlung. Fourteen! Small child to the
eye clinic. Loctite superglue."

"Copy."

Brenner's partner today was Hansi Munz. And needless
to say, whoever's not driving's manning the radio.

"Up and at 'em, gentlemen!" fat Nuttinger said, having
a bit of fun at their expense over the radio now. Because he
knew that Brenner and Munz had been there at the Kellerstüberl, too, last night.

"Kiss my ass," Munz replied. But needless to say, he wasn't
pressing the speak-button on the microphone anymore.

Just as they were delivering the kid who'd glued his eyes
shut to the clinic, the next run was already coming in over
the radio, a dialysis patient, and then a diabetic shock, and
then a motorcycle accident, and by the time they returned
to the station, it was already three-thirty in the afternoon.

Their colleagues in the crew room, though, weren't looking as cheery as they had that morning. Because one after
another, Junior was summoning all parties involved in the

Kellerstüberl incident the night before to his office. And it just so happened to be Munz's turn now.

While Brenner waited out in the hallway because he was up next, Lil' Berti sidled up to him, grinning: "You were there, too, last night, eh?"

"What is this, kindergarten? Where you've got to answer for every little orgy?"

"Might as well be. The others have all come out of Junior's office acting awfully sheepish and quiet."

"Even Bimbo?"

"When Bimbo was in there, Junior was shouting so loud that you could make out nearly every word from the crew room."

"All because of Angelika? Since when is Junior such a moralist?"

"Less because of Angelika. More because of Bimbo. Little by little, he's just been getting too cocky for Junior."

"Now, all the sudden?"

"Ever since he was in the newspaper. Bimbo just can't be stopped anymore. A couple of nurses in the geriatric ward have already filed a complaint about him."

"Is he snagging up seniors now?"

"It's the patients that are geriatric—not the nurses."

And seconds later, over the intercom came: "Herr Brenner, to the chief's office, please."

Munz ran into him on the stairs: "Have fun," he said, his vocal chords wobbling.

But when Brenner walked into the boss's office, big surprise.

Junior didn't bite his head off one bit. Quite the opposite.

He even offered him a seat—and so politely that you'd have thought Brenner was one of the five bearers of the golden responder badge. Because the silver responder badges are for EMTs, but golden—for paramedics only, and if you knew that a paramedic's ambulance is nothing more than an operating room on wheels, you'd start to grasp why you can count the number of living organ donors on one hand.

A few framed photos were hanging on the walls behind Junior, in which his father could be seen with various prominent people. The old man had been dead three years already, but it probably would've seemed disrespectful for Junior to swap the photos out for some of his own.

Even the pope was in one, from his trip to Vienna a few years ago when he blessed the ambulances. The pope had a little dust on his lips, but not because he'd kissed the runway at Schwechater airport, but because the glass in the frame hadn't been dusted in some time. You could tell from the man standing next to the pope. He also had dust on his face. But dust or no dust: you've never seen such a proud, contented smile as that of the old Rapid Response boss at the papal blessing of his fleet.

From some of the older drivers' stories and from Frau Aigner in accounting, Brenner knew that the old man had been a real you-know-what. How best to explain it? You've got to picture him a little like those Japanese. Who after fifty years in the jungle still refuse to believe that World War II is over. That's how the old man upheld his militarism at the EMS. Roll call, commanding tone of voice, the works. And if you don't have black socks on with your uniform: death penalty.

That's just an expression among the drivers for when, as a disciplinary measure, you get dispatched to a week of blood-donor duty out in the provinces—and it remains the most feared death penalty even today. But these days you only get it for severe violations, like when the shop boss overlooked a broken tailpipe on the 590 a couple weeks ago, and the exhaust found its way in to the patient in the back of the box. Or the DUI two years ago, where Hansi Munz didn't properly close the sliding door, and then, on the on-ramp to the autobahn, he lost a wheelchair—together with its patient—but Munz, in his stupor, didn't notice and kept on driving. The patient, thank god, dead on the spot, but Hansi Munz, needless to say, banished to the Waldviertel, one whole week, blood donations. But like I said: with the old man you'd have got that for a pair of white socks.

On the face of things, Junior was the spitting image of his old man. Except that the old man didn't have a mustache. And Junior's mustache was one of those sharp wedges that you could've uncapped your beer bottle on at any given moment.

You'd like to think a classic cop-stache like that wouldn't seem all that unusual to an ex-cop like Brenner. But given the resemblance between father and son, suddenly Junior's mustache wedge looked to Brenner like it'd been glued on. And once it seems like a person's mustache has been glued on, it's only a matter of time before their character comes to seem a little glued on, too, i.e. one big boss performance.

And so Brenner starts in on the profile now: voice too confident, gaze too steely, gait too swaggering. And the way he'd just cleaned house, of course, too sweeping.

But I guess Brenner just wanted to trot out his psychology know-how a little. Because the old man in the photos, well—he let it go. Although I have to admit, next to the pope, he almost looked more papal than the pope himself.

And he even cut a good figure next to the mayor of Vienna. Well, not next to the current mayor, who anybody'd cut a good figure next to. Next to the old mayor, though, him with the wife. You know, back when that hussy from the Prater was going as the mayor's wife for a while.

Junior noticed that Brenner was looking at the photos, and promptly said: "As a charitable organization, we constantly find ourselves perched in the public eye. We simply can't afford such escapades."

Brenner just nodded silently. He still thought Junior was talking about the whole incident at the Kellerstüberl.

"We've got enough problems as it is," Junior said now, as if by "we" he meant Junior and Brenner, and it was all them others that were the problem. After each sentence, Junior always looked back up at the ceiling, a strange habit, and Frau Aigner from accounting once told Brenner that Junior had adopted the gesture from his old man.

But you see, with things like this, it's all in the details. With the old man, maybe it'd looked statesmanlike. Brenner imagined his widespread hands touching only at the fingertips, while he read off some message like he was the Austrian chancellor.

With Junior, though, the opposite effect. Because he just looked like a bomber pilot in peak physical condition with a wedge for a mustache—or at least for as long as his head was bowed and he was looking up at you from below. But when you've got a cop-stache like his and you lift your head up, the person sitting across from you sees your mustache from below. Instead of smart mustachioed angles, all the sudden you're seeing thousands of hair follicles like on a broom. And a mustache from below, needless to say, always a sign of weakness.

"Will you join me for a glass of cognac?"

"I've still got to drive today."

Because A of all, Brenner had never drunk cognac before anyway, and B of all, trick question, of course.

"You won't be driving much more today," Junior said, glancing at his aviator's watch, and then he conjured two glasses and a bottle of cognac atop his desk. He poured and held his glass out to Brenner's for a toast: "*Zum Wohl.*"

Christ Almighty! There's nothing worse than when your boss wants to fraternize with you. And you know for a fact that he's trying to accomplish something by it, but he thinks you're too stupid to notice.

"I heard that Pro Med pinched an unconscious man right out from under you at the train station the other day."

"On account of the S-code, we didn't drive lights-and-sirens. And by the time we got there, he was already gone."

"You're not at fault," Junior said, interrupting Brenner's defense. "But this whole issue with Pro Med's getting worse and worse."

"I've heard that something like this has happened a few times already."

"Yes, it's happening more and more that they're stealing our injured right out from under us. Those are the methods of a robber baron."

Brenner didn't say anything to that.

"Now, I ask you, how is this possible?"

Junior looked up at the heavens and waited for a reply. But the heavens didn't say anything. And Brenner didn't say anything, either.

"You don't want to say it, but you know that there's only one explanation for this. You were, after all, a detective."

Brenner didn't say anything.

"Pro Med's tapping our radio," Junior said, snatching the answer right out from under him with an artfully furrowed brow.

Brenner had the feeling like he was expected to say something again now. But at the same time, his Latin teacher from Puntigam High appeared to him. "*Si tacuisses, philosophus mantises!*" the professor used to bark at every opportunity, roughly translated: Silence is golden. Because he used to have a good post at the Gestapo and now he was just a Latin teacher, making the window panes rattle all day long by demanding silence.

But Brenner had already said it—it'd just slipped out. Three times he'd remained silent and withheld the detective's stock phrase. But the fourth time he took Junior's bait with the story about the radio, and he said:

"Is there any proof?"

And you see, you should never overestimate a sign of weakness. Because Junior looked up at the heavens and, with a sympathetic mustache-smile, he said: "That's what I'd like for you to find out, Brenner."

CHAPTER 4

The next day at work, Brenner came down with a bad case of the mopes. And I still get a kick out of it today that it was Czerny of all people who had to bear the brunt of it. Czerny was famous for his mustache, which looked more like a goulash-colored toothbrush, and twist of fate: despite the toothbrush on his face, he had terrible bad breath. And believe it or not: that was the most likable thing about him.

Because there was only one topic that Czerny could talk about, and that was money. And if you talked to him for more than five minutes, guaranteed, he'd be hitting you up to buy some insurance, or a subscription to something. Except he never played poker, because Czerny's motto: multiplying wealth intelligently, *ja*, game of chance, *nein*.

But even five minutes would've been impossible with Brenner today. He was giving off the mopes so bad that Czerny didn't dare utter a word that first whole hour on the clock. It's often the money vultures who are the most sensitive people. Because you'll best be able to yank the shoes out from under a person, of course, if you can walk in their shoes a little first, i.e. empathy.

Czerny didn't even live at the Rapid Response Center, either, because he had his own place in Döblinger, the fancy neighborhood where all the villas are. A dialysis patient rented it out to him for a token schilling. The dialysis patients have to go to the hospital so frequently that as an EMT you automatically get to know them pretty well. And when Czerny found out that old Frau Dr. Kaspar owned several houses, he spun a charm that I've got to say, hats off. The patient hadn't even rejected her donated kidney yet before she was already rid of a villa.

"You're so monosyllabic today," Czerny eventually said.

"Monosyllabic?" Brenner answered.

A few minutes later, as they were waiting out front of the Brothers of Mercy, Czerny says:

"At least you're up to five now."

"Five what?"

"Five syllables that you said."

"Where'd I say five syllables?"

"Just now. When you said 'monosyllabic.' Monosyllabic. That's five syllables," the miser calculated. "So you can't say that you're monosyllabic."

"You're a minor philosopher, you know that?" Brenner grumbled.

"And you're a real sad sack. Junior must've reamed you out good yesterday."

Czerny couldn't have been more wrong, and yet he'd hit the nail right on the head: Junior was the cause of Brenner's mopes. Because Brenner had been so glad to have finally found an ordinary job. A routine and a salary and an apartment and a pension and everything. But the minute you don't watch out, already the past's caught up to you.

That would've been reason enough for Brenner's mopes.

That he should suddenly find himself playing detective for his boss. That he should suddenly find himself rummaging through other people's underwear again. Underwear, though, that's harmless enough. The worst for him was always the high-tech *Klimbim*. Even back on the force— radio? Never his thing. All those voices all the time. Brenner didn't even really know how a person was supposed to tap a radio. Never mind how he was supposed to tell if the Pro Meddlers were tapping theirs.

Tapping a tapper, that's just a perverse thought. If you're going to eavesdrop, then please, eavesdrop on what's being said, not what's being overheard. To eavesdrop on an eaves-dropper, though, that is just so completely wrong. Like when you're looking in a mirror that's also looking in a mirror. Maybe you know this game. And a ten-thousand-faceted-mirror-image storm clobbers you until you don't recognize yourself anymore.

It's almost like if you've ever thought about thinking. Try it sometime: while you're thinking, simultaneously think about your thinking! You'll see, the ganglia salad will be tossed sooner than you think.

I've been told that not even the brightest brain doctors know how they think. And that's why I can't explain it to you today, at least not in a generally applicable way. Because Brenner had his own methods. And for that I don't even need any medical jargon to explain Brenner's method of thinking to you. Because for his method, there's just one very simple word. And that word is "mopes."

And when Brenner had a problem that he couldn't solve, he fell into a slump that he couldn't climb back out of.

"What're your two cents about Junior still not letting us get any automatic transmissions installed?" Czerny said, trying to power through the lower depths of Brenner's mood a little.

Brenner, though, no comment. He even got a piece of gum out of the glove compartment, even though normally, never a gum-chewer. But today, demonstrably: I cannot talk because I need my mouth to chew.

"Last week," Czerny said, sticking it out a little longer, "I drove this real classy patient to Munich. Ten hours on the autobahn, let me tell you, if that's not hell on the right shoe. An automatic sure would've been a dream."

Brenner was chewing his gum so mightily that you'd have thought the battery had fallen out of the ambulance and he had to use his chew-muscles to generate his own backup power supply. "When I look at my shoes, my right shoe is worn out and all lopsided from accelerating. With an automatic, that'd be gone in an instant. Take a look at your shoes sometime!"

Over the course of his life, Brenner's moods had, more often than not, struck a nerve with others. But flip side of the coin: the more mopey he got about a problem, the more he dug his heels in.

That's why I say generating his own backup power supply. You've got to think of it like at a hospital where the power goes out. Needless to say, they've got an emergency backup generator, so that the most important equipment will be provided for. Because, power goes out, middle of an operation, good night. And with his store of backup power, Brenner could carry on his work with Czerny just like usual today. He didn't let the patients fall on the ground, he didn't intubate them in the gullet, and he didn't run anybody over, either.

Just backup power, though, not main power supply. Big question now: Where does the main power go when the power goes out? It doesn't just disappear, it's got to go somewhere. What did Brenner's brain do the whole time he was wheeling around on his backup-power slump for hours on end?

Not what you're thinking, though, he brought an un-swerving focus to his work, what with the high-voltage power lines that were being freed up. You don't know Brenner very well, then. Brenner was so prone to distraction that it was almost like you had to go searching for him. Sometimes it even seemed like a disability to him. The more important a problem was, the more distracted he got. That made his life on the police force rather difficult. And for this caliber of distractedness, you need a lot more energy, of course, than you do to concentrate just a little.

Brenner was thinking about a hundred thousand different things right now, just not about how he might solve the Pro Med radio problem. Pay attention, though, so you'll see why it's always been Brenner's distractedness, of all things, that's got him the bad guys in the end.

Because at half past four, he still hadn't wasted a single thought over Pro Med and the radio. Instead, besides the hundred thousand other things, Brenner thought of the photo of the pope in Junior's office. And how the pope had all that dust on his lips. And how Hansi Munz had once told him one of his never-ending jokes: how the pope once made a guest appearance on the TV show *Wanna Bet?* because he could tell all the airport runways apart by how they taste.

In his distractedness, Brenner was reminded of how they'd once arrested a peeping tom back when he was on the force. Vienna was his prowling grounds, but they picked him up in Tirol—on the run for the Italian border. He took off when the Vienna police found his surveillance rig. And nobody could believe it—he lived in an apartment complex with over a hundred units, and every single apartment was tapped. And at the time, the cops were always saying Oswald could go on *Wanna Bet?* and recognize every single woman in his apartment complex just from their moans.

Oswald. You see what I mean by this caliber of distractedness. How after twelve years Brenner flushed his name out right then and there.

"I've just got to stop by the bank real quick," Brenner said to his partner at four-thirty-three.

"Gotta make a deposit?"

Unbelievable, that Czerny. Nothing but money on his mind. But Brenner's mopes had completely vanished now. He didn't need it anymore—I mean what I explained to you before about the backup generator. And now: problem solved, mopes *adieu*, that was Brenner's way.

Czerny waited in the vehicle, and when Brenner came back out, he told his partner they'd be returning to the station.

"Return to station? We've still got three runs to make before we can return. If we're lucky."

"Seven-seventy return to station!" came over the radio at just that moment, though, and that made Czerny look pretty dumb. He couldn't have known that Brenner had this special assignment from Junior. Nor could he have known that Brenner had only ducked into the bank in order to call fat Nuttinger back at the dispatch center.

You're going to say, Why didn't he just radio in from the ambulance? But then everybody would've heard it, you didn't think about that, did you? Including Pro Med. And you see, it's the little things that make the detective. He finds himself a stinking phone booth, whereas the likes of us might prefer to make a show of it and radio in to fat Nuttinger.

When Brenner got back to his apartment, he spent another solid hour on the phone, and by half past eight, he was already sitting in Café Augarten.

And at quarter to nine, Herr Oswald came in. In his elegant suit, Brenner didn't recognize him at first. Because in just twelve years, Herr Oswald had aged about thirty.

Above all, it was his white hair that did it. Upon closer inspection you would've seen that he wasn't all that old. And when Brenner offered him his hand, he saw that, from up close, it wasn't that Oswald looked unnaturally old, but just unnaturally oversensitive.

Because, these days, if voyeurism's your bag, you're going to tend to err on the sensitive side.

So it didn't surprise Brenner one bit when Herr Oswald read his thoughts. "I'm an old man," was the first thing Oswald said.

"How old are you?"

"Fifty-one."

"That's nothing today," Brenner said, patronizingly, as though he, Brenner, were decades away from fifty.

"I don't have a problem with it," Herr Oswald said with a sensitive smile. "It was my younger years that were a problem for me, anyhow. You know which ones I'm talking about."

"I wouldn't want to be young again, either, today," Brenner claimed.

Herr Oswald ordered himself a mineral water. In this grotty café on the outskirts of town, the elegant Herr fit in about as well as a swallowed piece of evidence does in your intestinal flora. "For some time now, peace, praise god, has returned to my life. I've been married nine years. And the aberrations of my youth, owing to which you first made my acquaintance, belong even farther in the past."

The aberrations of youth, owing to which you first made my acquaintance. Brenner almost had to laugh at the old perv's stilted manner. "Did you even do any time back then?"

"Probation. And not due to my actual offenses." Herr Oswald spoke High German with a vengeance. "But rather, due to my resistance against the—well, you're aware. During the arrest."

Only now did Brenner remember how, there on the Italian border, he'd beaten out Herr Oswald's two incisors with his firearm until he finally surrendered.

"I already told you over the phone what I want from you. You're the foremost expert in bugging and tapping systems that I know, and—"

"And I already told you over the phone that I haven't had a trifle to do with any of that stuff in exactly twelve years."

The elegant, white-haired Herr got a little off balance there. I don't mean to suggest that he was getting angry, but his face changed color ever so slightly, and when he interrupted Brenner, a certain fierceness entered his voice. You'd have thought the gritty surroundings of the café were almost starting to rub off on the elegant Herr a little—the intestinal flora slowly getting to work on the swallowed photographic evidence, as it were.

A sip of mineral water, and immediately composed again. Brenner didn't say anything for a little while—he simply let the Café Augarten have its way with him a little.

Apart from the two of them and the waiter, there was only one other customer in the joint, a woman in a tracksuit going to town on the one-armed bandit. Even though the place was practically empty, it stank so bad of cigarette smoke that for a moment Brenner thought the schmaltzy Italian singer sounded even huskier than usual, and pronto, a coughing fit came over him.

"I only consented to meet you here because I didn't wish to speak about this over the phone with my wife there beside me."

"She doesn't know about the aberrations of your youth, owing to which we first became acquainted?"

Herr Oswald just gave Brenner's mockery a pitiful shake of his head.

"And your wife's not going to find anything out about it, either."

"Of course she won't. Namely, because there won't be any more contact between you and me. Namely, because I couldn't even help you if I wanted to. I wouldn't know from where to procure the equipment. I've nothing more to say."

The Italian cancer candidate was already on to the next song and still valiantly battling against a coughing fit.

And Herr Oswald was just being so sensitive that Brenner couldn't help but step on his toes a little now: "That piece of evidence that you swallowed back at the Reschenpass—"

The tall, slender Herr suddenly got a head shorter. And then: "You know all about it."

Amore, amore. Interesting, though, why the Italians should all have such good voices.

"I was on the horn earlier with Riedl."

"Then you know all about it."

And you see, that's why I say: Proper telephoning skills make up about fifty percent of detective work. Because in the few hours he'd had between five and eight, Brenner didn't just call Oswald, but also his former partner Riedl on the force, who'd detained Oswald in Tirol while Brenner tried to keep him from swallowing the photographic evidence. Riedl was still a cop and had looked into the case a little for Brenner, i.e. computer.

Brenner didn't have to list off the details for Herr Oswald now. How the medical examiner had produced the photographic evidence that Herr Oswald had swallowed— together with his two incisors—still half-digested. And that Herr Oswald would've been put behind bars at least two years for it. If he hadn't started working for the police as an informant in the meantime.

Because, for a perv, taking a couple of nice collector's photos is one thing, but becoming a tacit witness to such a crime, that's a whole 'nother page in the book—and a swallowed one at that.

From Riedl, Brenner had learned that Herr Oswald still

has the gear at his disposal today—compared to which all the gear on the state police is a tin-can phone at best, i.e. handicrafts for boys.

"Your wife won't hear anything about it," Brenner assured him.

"So what do you want from me?"

Brenner could see he was relieved.

"Tap a radio?" Herr Oswald almost laughed. "That's no problem," he said, and nearly choked on his mineral water.

Brenner was downright cheerful on his way home. He thought the worst was behind him for today. Hardly a case of exaggerated optimism, if you consider that it was only three minutes till midnight.

Nevertheless, mistaken. Because at the entrance to the Rapid Response Center, he ran into Hansi Munz, and Brenner could see right away that he was completely beside himself.

"Big's dead!"

Brenner could tell he wasn't joking. Because of the fact that he'd said "Big" and not "Bimbo," i.e. respect for the dead.

Nevertheless, he had to laugh for a second, as if Hansi Munz had told him a good joke.

CHAPTER 5

"I'd like to know what's so funny!" Hansi Munz yelled. "Death's big," Brenner answered. But Munz was still dumbfounded, of course: "Big's dead!" he repeated stubbornly. "Bimbo! I'd like to know what's so funny about that!"

"I'm not laughing," Brenner insisted. Because A of all, he really didn't see anything else funny now. And B of all, he just didn't have the patience to tell Munz the whole story. Definitely not in his condition. But I can fill you in real quick.

When you're an undertaker nowadays, well, that's a highly skilled profession. It's not like it used to be, where people would say: Sure, look a little sad, a couple hundred nails in the coffin, and *voilà*, an undertaker's already a made man. Tremendous job specifications: You've got to do psychology, you've got to do gardening, you've got to jump the bureaucratic hurdles, you've got to do all the bookkeeping. And, and, and!

And even that doesn't earn you a spot among the top morticians. Because the top guy's also got to know his literature: Japanese, Chinese, wisdom, the works.

When Brenner's aunt keeled over in line for the Easter confession some years ago, he was the one who had to pick out the words for the funeral program from the undertaker's

catalog. When the undertaker really had to hand it to
Brenner that what he'd picked out was truly the most beautiful in all the catalog, listen to this:

> "Death's big.
> We're his chuckling mouths.
> When we find ourselves
> In the middle of our lives
> He dares to rhyme
> Within us."

No, wait a minute:

> "He dares to cry
> Within us."

That's right. And to tell you the truth, if I were picking
out a poem for a funeral program today, I'd take that one,
too. Because, dares to cry, powerful. That's one you've got
to let fully dissolve on your tongue. You've got to watch out
that you yourself don't start crying, or even get a little, you
know. The bit about the "mouths" I like less, but that's probably the way it's got to be.

Now listen to this. The funeral for his aunt was over
ten years ago. And the poem was buried about as deep in
Brenner's head as his aunt was in the Puntigam Cemetery,
i.e. completely decomposed. Unreal, though, when Hansi
Munz says to Brenner at midnight, "Big's dead," the complete poem rose up from the grave, not unlike Angelika's
hair the night before—witching hour, no mistake.

And to tell you the truth, I can understand why Brenner wouldn't have any desire to tell Munz the whole story. Because he wanted to finally learn how Big died.

Unfortunately, though. One word begets the next. And as they entered the courtyard, Hansi Munz, still furious: "You definitely laughed!"

And I don't know, was it the unsettling mood in the courtyard, this unnatural middle-of-the-night atmosphere, the whole place abuzz with excitement—even though only the 8Ks worked nights, and not a single one of them lived there—or did Brenner just down one beer too many at the Café Augarten and that's why he said to Hansi Munz now:

"Death's big, we're his chuckling mouths."

"What the hell are you talking about?"

"Ack, nothing. What happened to Big?"

"Did you say 'Munz'?" Hansi Munz wouldn't let up, though.

"I didn't say 'Munz.' I said 'mouths.' It's like a poem."

And so he did have to explain the whole story about the poem to Munz after all. By the time Munz was finally satisfied, though, they'd already made their way over to the dispatch center, where an 8K named Fürstauer was presiding.

If it's unusual for one of the full-timers to talk to an 8K, then, it goes without saying, completely unimaginable for the 8K to be the one giving the full-timers the lowdown. Needless to say, it was eerie now: midnight, a dead man in the garage, and an 8K in the know.

"Shall I perhaps repeat everything one more time now?" Fürstauer asked Brenner, making no effort to hide his irritation. Because Fürstauer was a clever guy, he knew for a fact that he wouldn't be the star forever. And so you've got to get a move on with the airs and graces if you're going to get something out of this now.

"Where'd you find him, then?"

"At nine-twenty p.m. the emergency call came in," volunteer Fürstauer said, starting back at Adam and Eve.

"Code Twelve, motorcycle accident. Mraz was my partner. He's being questioned up in the training room by the police as we speak. Even though I've already told them everything. And way better than Mraz could've. Before I switched to VISTAA, I was an elementary school teacher for eleven years. And the one thing the children did not and would not comprehend: the difference between a summary and a full account. But I still managed to drum it into every one of them. At the end of their schooling, every one of my kids knew: summary, five lines max—or, hey, maybe even one line—okay, six, if one of them had large handwriting. And the converse: full account—with details, too."

"Give it a try with the summary, Fürstauer."

Fürstauer reminded Brenner a little of the gym teacher that he'd had in high school back in Puntigam. A nearly identical bald head, and just like Fürstauer, the gym teacher let his hair grow long on the left and then slicked it over to his right ear. A cunning solution really, except that when the gym teacher ran even a single step, the sheer effort would cause his hair to loosen from his head and hang down all lopsided on his left shoulder.

And as Brenner needled him about the summary just now, he had the distinct impression that volunteer Fürstauer's slicked-over skull hairs had loosened a little, too. As if his spit had lost its sticking power at that exact moment. Definitely couldn't have been the insult that made his hair bristle. Must've just been the night breeze, tousling Fürstauer's hair all the sudden.

"I don't have to tell you anything," Fürstauer said with a frosty air that reminded Brenner of how chilly it can suddenly feel at night even in June.

But like I said. Fürstauer was a clever guy—if he wasn't, he wouldn't have made it all the way to being an elementary school teacher. Pedagogical Academy and everything. And then, even switched to VISTAA. If you ask me, he should've stayed a teacher. But, character assassination story, unfortunately. No sooner had he finished drumming it into all the kids than they went to the police and provided a full account—with details, too.

Then again, that was fifteen years ago. And he hadn't been encircled by a flock of interested listeners since. He wasn't going to let a little goading ruin his fun now. And after a brief moment of silence, like he was letting an impertinent pupil stew for a bit, he continued with his story.

"When we arrived at the accident site, needless to say, first things first, get out the vac-mat. Because with motorcyclists, you never know about the spinal column, and I never do anything without a vac-mat. Maybe he's lying fresh on the asphalt, happy as a clam, you think, he's only had a slight shock, and a second later, he's a paraplegic because you handled him wrong. And on the vac, he gets poured right in, like wax into a mold.

"So that's why I always see my motorcyclists on TV a year later in the wheelchair Olympics," Hansi Munz inter-griped now, "because I always forget the vac." Because it'd got to the point that an 8K's telling you how to do your job.

But Fürstauer didn't let it rattle him: "With motorcyclists, always the vac, I say. In a normal case. Today, though, anything but normal. I fling open the tailgate on the seven-forty so I can get the vac out—only to discover that the vac was already occupied. If it wasn't for his uniform, I wouldn't have even recognized Bimbo."

Such an embittered expression came over his face that he even had to spit, and then he said: "Just once I'd like to hear what a uniform critic might have to say about that."

You should know, in the Emergency Services field, time and again there were uniform critics.

Okay, not among the EMTs themselves, but nurses, let's say, or these hippie male nurses who have to spend their days shaving pubes, while their own full beards have never even seen a pair of scissors. At the end of the day, though, mouths flapping wide open and playing the part of uniform critic.

Among the men themselves, this kind of thing doesn't happen, of course. And the whole time Senior was in charge, it goes without saying, the uniform critics didn't have a chance. And just between us: uniform renunciation would've been the death of every EMS organization out there. Because most of the volunteers were only there on account of the uniforms. Fürstauer was no exception.

"At first, I thought Bimbo was just sleeping off a hangover on the vac. Because let's be honest, it wouldn't have been the first time that something like that's happened."

"Which isn't for you to say."

"But then," the old schoolteacher said, ignoring Hansi

Munz, "I was struck right away by how red Bimbo's head was. Now, granted, Bimbo's head was always relatively red. But needless to say, a head as red as this, and eyes as red and bulging as these, and a tongue rolled up all the way over his mustache like that one was? Never, not even in one of his drunken stupors, did Bimbo look like that. And as a matter of fact, it wasn't from alcohol poisoning. It was from the millimeter-thin line of blood that Bimbo had around his neck—that must've been one extremely thin wire. I immediately called it in: Big's dead."

Big. Not: Bimbo. And from this point forward, everybody only said Big, nobody said Bimbo anymore. Because, like I said, respect for the dead.

"Since when's an Eight-K allowed to determine a death?" Munz said, giving the chain another rattle.

Fürstauer, though—100-percent Pedagogical Academy—simply ignored his ill-behaved listener: "The dispatch center then sent a backup ambulance for the motorcyclist, but, by the time they finally got there, the motorcyclist was already back on his feet. And if the police hadn't forced him to take a Breathalyzer, he would've got right back on his bent-up bike."

"He probably had another tour bus to jump over," a young 8K dryly inserted there. His voice was still changing and he didn't even have a respectable mustache yet. No downy facial hair, either, like Hansi Munz, just individual strands of hair like a pig hide ready for tanning, or like that city councilman in charge of transit, you know, Svihalek. He was trying hard to come up with an even dryer line now. But not a chance, because Munz was back to his jabbering:

"Have the Eight-Ks completely lost it now? Since when's an Eight-K allowed to determine a death? What's happened to radio protocol?"

"Radio protocol?" Fürstauer spat out scornfully, and then he played his greatest trump: "Maybe if you'd seen Big ..."

Because needless to say, nobody there had seen him. "When we sat him up, his tongue was hanging down to his knees."

"Like that woman I once drove with the gunshot to the knee," Hansi Munzi cackled. "Suicide attempt! Because she'd asked her doctor ahead of time where the heart is. And what do you guys think he said?"

"This is an old joke," Brenner grumbled.

"Two centimeters beneath the nipple," Hansi Munz howled.

Suddenly it seemed to Brenner as if the ghost of Bimbo had wandered into Hansi Munz's body, because usually only Bimbo talked this much nonsense. And while Brenner was still thinking about whether that sort of thing's even possible, he asked Fürstauer: "Where's Big now?"

"Still in the seven-forty. The cops sealed up the garage and left Bimbo lying there for the time being so that no clues get tampered with."

I've got to hand it to them, though, incredible. They sealed up that garage door so superbly that you'd have thought the whole place would collapse if somebody tore the tape down. The small doorway connecting the 730 garage to the 740, though, that they didn't tape off.

A second later and Fürstauer's five minutes of fame had already passed. For a while there, he'd been the only one who'd seen Bimbo dead. Because, needless to say, half the crew followed Brenner into the 730 garage and through the narrow connecting door over to the 740. Only the most dutifully timid of volunteers didn't dare.

But then, when Brenner opened the door to the 740, the first wave turned back, and then, when he climbed in and unzipped Bimbo's body bag, there were just six of them left in the garage. Because, needless to say, Junior or the cops, who were up on the second floor questioning Mraz in the training room, they could turn up at any second.

And then, as Brenner started examining Bimbo, there were only four of them left.

"I wouldn't do that," Fürstauer said frantically, as Brenner went about palpating Bimbo's neck. Fürstauer still thought that Brenner just wanted a closer look at the wound. He couldn't have known that he was just moments away from watching Brenner drive his fingers a full centimeter deep into the wafer-thin wound like some kind of Asian miracle healer.

Fürstauer was silent with fright. And Horak didn't say anything, either. And neither did Hansi Munz.

But they didn't puke, either. Although it was definitely a major test of their self-control when Brenner fished the gold chain out from Bimbo's neck.

"Monk and nun," Brenner said.

"You writing poems again?" At first, Hansi Munz thought Brenner might be in shock. But, needless to say, a well-known fact that people who are in shock often believe that other people are in shock.

"That's why the gold chain didn't break off," Brenner explained.

"Monk and nun," Hansi Munz echoed back, stunned.

"Did Bimbo never regale you with how his latest gold chain was made? He went on and on about it to everybody: not just links joined together any which way. No, monk and nun method. Just like interlocking roof tiles."

"Why's it called 'monk and nun'?"

"I'll give you three guesses. Because the one part's got a slot, and the other's got a pin that sticks out."

"And this is something special?"

"You can see it didn't break, can't you? Even though it's this thin. Bimbo said you could hang a grand from it."

"A gram doesn't weigh anything."

"He said a *grand*, a piano."

"And you knew about this? That makes you look like you did it."

Brenner carefully fished out the gold chain from all around Bimbo's neck until it was draped neatly back along his collarbone like in Bimbo's better days. "Do you still remember how Lil' Berti explained to Bimbo that the grime came from his neck?"

"Yeah, so?"

Brenner pointed at the blood-smeared gold chain. "Well, today the grime really did come from his neck."

"Lil' Berti didn't mean it that way, though. Otherwise, it's look like he did it."

"Everybody looks like they did it, as far as you're concerned."

"That's the damn thing about a thing like this. From the get-go, everybody's a suspect. That's why I'm glad they've already got somebody."

Brenner was just thinking that dead Bimbo was looking

pretty bad. But now he himself looked even worse. "What did you say? Who've they got?"

"Lanz."

And then, a hailstorm, the likes of which would've had you thinking: in all twenty-three of Vienna's precincts, twenty-seven had simultaneously erupted, i.e. all able-bodied men to the rescue. Because to the cops, it truly was a catastrophe to discover somebody giving their corpse a working-over.

There were four of them, two in uniform and two in sports coats. Interesting, though! Even though they were both wearing practically identical sports coats, you could still tell which one was the boss by his coat. But maybe it wasn't just the coat. Because needless to say, the boss was also the one who wasn't shouting. In their world, it's the deputy who does the shouting.

"ID!" the deputy shouted.

"I'll just run get it. I live just upstairs here at the station."

"No way! You're coming with us."

"You can only take me in if I'd gone through the taped-off door. But you forgot the side door. That's something you learn Day One from Franzi: 'Adjathent doorth and windowth, likewithe, theal 'em off,'" Brenner said, imitating the lisp of Hofrat Franzmeier, who'd been the director of cadet training for a good twenty years.

The next shout remained lodged in the deputy's throat. The fact that the side door hadn't been taped off, needless to say, his mistake. He didn't dare glance over at his boss right now. And the mention of Franzi told him the rest.

In a situation like this, though, a boss has got to rein in

his subordinate and hold off on telling him off until later. "Former colleagues who mix themselves up in our work are our absolute favorites," he said sarcastically.

But when Brenner showed him the gold chain on Bimbo's neck, he simmered down.

"How did you know that?" the deputy found his tongue again.

"He always wore one. That's why I looked for it. But it wasn't all that hard to find, because under his collar there in the back, a chunk of it was still sticking out."

There are certain types of bosses who are unable to nod. Not because their necks are that thick, but because they're too good to nod, i.e. you'd have to grow another foot and a half before we're on nodding terms; i.e. it's nodding enough if I just stare vacantly into your eyes for two seconds instead of bawling you down another couple of inches.

And when those two seconds were over, the cop in the boss coat withdrew his glossy choleric eyes from Brenner and ordered his uniformed colleagues to book Lanz and then take Bimbo to autopsy.

"And you stay here and watch out that these nutjobs don't tamper with the evidence," he said to his sports-coat twin.

Back outside, Junior was dispersing everybody from the courtyard, i.e. What I'd like to do most is take my new Raab Kärcher–brand high-pressure hose to this whole mess. Brenner was just glad that he could slip away to his apartment now amid the general confusion.

"Brenner," Junior said, as Brenner went past him. Nothing else, just: "Brenner."

As he unlocked the door to his apartment, Brenner was still contemplating whether that had been a greeting or a threat or a cry for help.

He didn't contemplate it long, though. Because he saw that somebody had slipped a handwritten note under his door. "Please call me: 47."

Now, you're probably thinking, 47's a response code. And you wouldn't be completely wrong, because if you ask me, the telephone truly is an event to be responded to. But listen up to what I'm telling you.

They used to have to call each other with a regular phone system, and so they had to pay the regular fees for calls. But then, when they got the new dispatch center, it came with a new phone network, too. Junior let all of them in the building switch to internal extensions, and ever since, they've been able to talk on the phone for hours with each other, and it doesn't cost them a schilling. And 47 was Lanz's extension.

Even though Brenner had just seen the uniforms drive off with Lanz, he dialed the number anyway.

"Lanz residence."

"Your father slipped a note under my door," Brenner said to Angelika.

"That wasn't my father. It was me."

"What did you want to talk to me about?"

"Could you maybe pop by and see me?"

As he left his apartment, he could already hear a door opening upstairs, and before he even got there, Angelika had already turned on the light in the hall for him. The Lanz apartment was just one floor above his own.

Even in her sweatpants, Angelika was wearing her belt with the gold buckle that had the letters "ESCAPADE" emblazoned on it, which Brenner had never seen her without. And you'd see her pretty often during the day, because it was only in the evening that she waited tables somewhere.

"Did you get off work early tonight?" Brenner asked, in that way that you say something when you're paying a visit to a woman in the middle of the night so that it doesn't get awkward.

She didn't say moo or baa, though, just held the door open to Brenner and showed him to the kitchen, which was exactly as small as Brenner's was.

"Want something to drink? I only have coffee, though."

"No, thanks." Brenner was beginning to feel ill anyway just from the fluorescent overhead light, which lit up the kitchenette like an operating room. Or maybe you shouldn't always blame everything on poor fluorescent lights. Maybe it was a side effect of his gold-chain post-mortem.

"Coffee at this hour," Angelika said, with an apologetic smile. "But it doesn't have any effect on me. And I'm not getting any sleep tonight anyway."

"What happened to your father?"

She had this way of smoking where every drag made a centimeter-deep hollow in her cheeks. As if the situation were flipped, i.e. the whole kitchenette was full of life-endangering flue gases, and it was only through the filter of her Kim that a little oxygen would get in.

She didn't sit down with Brenner at the table, but leaned against the refrigerator so that there were three, four meters between the two of them. "They think he strangled Big."

"What does your father say to that?"

"I don't know. They took him away before I could see him."

"Does he have a lawyer?"

"Junior called the company lawyer."

"Do you think he did it?"

She shook her head. Very slowly, as if she didn't want to shake her head so much as sniff the air to see in what direction the truth might lie, like in an animal documentary on TV.

And only when her Kim was smoked down to the filter did she say: "Those idiots think he did it on account of the other night in the Kellerstüberl."

Brenner didn't quite know where he should look. On the inside, he was nodding. But on the outside, he didn't nod. And all the sudden he realized that he was doing it exactly like the boss cop in the sports coat did. Not even nodding. Just staring, obstinately, straight ahead.

If it hadn't been for the sports-coat cop, it never would've occurred to him that he was playing the dopey no-nodder to Angelika. But now that it had occurred to him, he quickly said: "So that's why they immediately took him away."

"Bimbo was provoking him all the time."

"Yeah, so? You don't just go and kill somebody for that."

Angelika assumed her thoughtful animal-documentary mien. I'm no Doctor Doolittle from TV, but if I had to translate that look, I would guess that Angelika was using her animal look to say: I'm not so sure that somebody wouldn't strangle Bimbo for that.

But in fact, all she said was: "That's not all. My father drove the seven-forty with Bimbo today."

Brenner didn't nod. Not even on the inside.

"But in spite of all that, it wasn't him that did it," Angelika said, as she lit up her next Kim with a "Give the Gift of Life: Donate Blood" lighter.

Fluorescent lights notwithstanding, Angelika seemed much prettier than usual today to Brenner. And when you're on the force, you'll come to make this observation time and again. The first time it struck Brenner was when his colleague Knoll's wife was killed in an accident. That was still in his uniform days, so, over fifteen years ago. A petite, funny Carinthian, good skier, but always went too fast behind the wheel. I think she enjoyed it—that as the wife of a police officer, she could just tear up her speeding tickets.

After the accident, Brenner was struck by how his colleague changed. That probably sounds somehow, I don't know. The only way I can put it is this: the sadness somehow made Knoll beautiful. Knoll of all people, who even a simpleton could see that, apart from skiing and TV, nothing whatsoever in his skull—and fat, too, only thirty-five years old.

Over the years, Brenner would be struck by this again and again. This aura that despairing people had. With Knoll, though, the aura quickly evaporated again. After a year of mourning, he married a hairstylist. And needless to say, hair dryer, not good for the aura.

Angelika Lanz had terrible beauty-shop hair, too. You've seen it before: dyed and permed a thousand times.

A long, withered shag that had never known nature outside the beauty shop that'd chemically produced it.

And yet, Brenner was unable to detect any of the usual

trashiness that Angelika radiated. A beautiful, sad woman. With an aura, Brenner thought to himself. And with a cigarette. And a question.

"Didn't you used to be a detective?" Shit, Brenner thought. Just don't nod.

CHAPTER 6

It's a law: If you don't have anybody to love, you must search for all eternity until you find somebody. No sooner will you find them, though, than three more will parade past you later that same day. Now to apply this law to the detective: no sooner had Brenner chucked the detective work than every day seemed to present him with a new client.

Brenner didn't necessarily have the feeling that Junior's and Angelika's cases could be settled all that easily, either. And stuck between two chairs like that, well, you know how the saying goes, always the danger that your hemorrhoids will catch a chill.

It wasn't until the next day, when he got summoned to Junior's shortly before four, that he noticed how bad Junior looked. There are people who always look bad, for whom it's a good sign if you can detect violet rings under their eyes. Because that means they didn't drink through the night for once, and so a little color's returned to their faces in contrast to the rings. But when a person who places as much importance on health and fitness as the young Rapid Response boss generally does suddenly looks like one of the drug addicts that the EMTs transport to the emergency room, then, needless to say, alarm.

Today's mustache was not the sharp wedge that you could uncap your beer bottle on. Bomber pilot no more. Droopy, even. A little like that popular philosopher, hold on, what's his name again, quick, the one with the whip. You know, mustache like a seal, the kind where it gets a little tricky with the food bits. Where you've got to smuggle your *consommé Cèlestine* past the old soup-strainer.

Interesting, though, how often the exterior matches the interior! Because it wasn't just Junior's mustache that went droopy overnight, but he was also prattling on rather philo-sophically today:

"The International Committee of the Red Cross is one of our civilization's greatest achievements."

And even if you forget everything else, one thing I'd like to impart on your life's journey: When a person goes on as sanctimoniously as this, you can always assume that he's got something to hide. Now, Brenner knew right away, of course, that Junior didn't want to admit how much of a toll Bimbo's death was taking on him. Just like Hansi Munz had been unbearably mouthy last night so as not to let anything show, Junior was carrying on sanctimoniously now.

"The mission of the International Committee of the Red Cross is exactly one hundred and thirty-nine years old."

Needless to say now, Battle of Solferino, senseless blood-bath, Henri Dunant, whole shebang. He really didn't need to tell Brenner all this. Because Brenner had already heard it ten times a day during EMT training. Understandable, then, that Brenner should meander a bit in his thoughts. All those French names start to sound alike—Henri Dunant, Brigitte Bardot, and, and, and.

"But do you know what's inextricably linked to the mission of the International Committee of the Red Cross?"

Pay attention to what I'm telling you. Because was I not just talking about the often uncanny link between the philosophical mustache and philosophical talk? Well, incredible: first, thought-digression onto French names—and now, the French experience. Because Brenner was having such a case of déjà vu right now that the plastic seat under his rear practically dematerialized.

All the sudden he was back sitting on one of the wooden chairs at the police academy, where they were always beating you over the head with these old truisms, too. "The executive branch is one of the three pillars of democracy." Brenner heard this sentence so often at the police academy that he automatically assumed it wasn't true at the time—a regular contrarian, as it were. And the things he'd go on to experience while still in law enforcement, well, I don't even want to get started now, or else you might leap right off this bridge of mine.

The use of force by the police, though, always plenty to discuss—and important for you young people to discuss it, too. Just like it's important for the hamster to gnaw its teeth down on the bars of its cage. The hamster that Brenner's grandfather gave him when he was a kid always did that, too.

"The International Committee of the Red Cross," Junior said, startling Brenner, who was still annoyed about how the sound of that damn hamster-rattling used to keep him from falling asleep, "is only conceivable through one-hundred-percent impartiality on the part of the International Committee of the Red Cross. The International Committee of the Red Cross must be neutral. It's the only way in which we can care for the injured on both sides of war. One-hundred-percent neutrality. *Tutti Fratelli* was Henri Dunant's motto. Brothers all."

"Yeah, yeah, or else the warring parties won't let us into all the blockade zones."

"That's right. Throughout the whole world, Angola, Mozambique, wherever you look. No diplomacy, no nothing. Just one-hundred-percent neutrality."

As a matter of fact, practically every other day there was a story in the newspapers about how the Red Cross's neutrality wasn't exactly a hundred percent. But Brenner decided not to say anything. Sometimes boss-people just need to mechanically recite the sermons that they themselves don't even believe in. And Brenner thought to himself, Junior just doesn't want to admit that Bimbo's death is taking a toll on him.

But then Junior took Brenner by surprise when suddenly he got concrete: "You took the GED, you must know what happened in 1934."

What's this all about? At first Junior's line of questioning just provoked Brenner. Are we back in school or something? Am I going to get quizzed on dates?

But when you get worked up, the body emits certain substances, and with these substances, your memory functions better.

"Civil war in Austria," Brenner answered, like a shot from a pistol.

But instead of Junior praising him, he looked about as dismayed as if the answer had been false. It wasn't Brenner's answer that troubled him, though. It was the implications of it: "In the civil war, we, in Vienna, lost our neutrality. The Fascists dissolved the Red Cross. And so we weren't able to look after our wounded workers. That was a dreadful mistake. That was madness."

"Workers have got their own unions again these days. In fact, Pro Med's got—"

"That's what's madness!" Junior snarled at Brenner. Actually, I'd have to call it flying off the handlebar. Because, in his rage, his mustache, which Junior had let droop so philosophically at first, was now standing at pert attention again. And it wouldn't surprise me if the roots of the hairs weren't stimulated by the adrenaline, kind of like with fertilizer. "That's exactly what's so mad! That's the sheer madness of it, Brenner!"

The workers wouldn't have lived to see today anyway, Brenner thought.

And then, quite softly, Junior said: "And our organization won't survive for long, either, not if Pro Med continues like it has been."

Brenner didn't say anything.

"Say something."

"What am I supposed to say?"

"I lost two of my most capable men yesterday, and that's all you can come up with?"

Nice and slowly, he was starting to turn aggressive. Philosophical at first, but now a bit more aggressive, nice and slow. Brenner knew that he'd reveal in his own sweet time what he'd actually been wanting to say all along.

"The one killed. And the other arrested." Junior sighed

and took off his glasses. He wore such odd reading glasses—they didn't go with the muscled physique at all. About as little as the silver chain that he always wore on his right wrist. But if you're going to look at it that way, then, the whole desk was out of place. Junior was rumored to still go out on calls, but by himself, the lone medic. And then, needless to say, no reading glasses, no, only sunglasses.

"That's all you can come up with?" he muttered again from behind the hand that he was using to massage the bridge of his nose with.

"Maybe it wasn't Lanz at all. I could see if I can find anything out."

Junior shook his head, exasperated: "Are you listening to me at all, Brenner?"

"You've got no doubts that Lanz did it?" Brenner said, playing dumb a little, because he was curious to see if Junior would get even more concrete with his suspicions about Pro Med.

"I know he didn't do it," Junior said to the ceiling again, as if he were reconnecting with his higher power. "But at this very moment, I couldn't care less about old Lanz. This here isn't about Lanz. It's about the survival of our entire organization!"

"It almost sounds as if you believe it was Pro Med that's behind Bimbo's—" Junior gave him such a strange look that Brenner immediately corrected himself—"behind paramedic Big's murder."

"It's okay, you can say 'Bimbo.'" He stole a brief look up at the ceiling, but evidently there was nothing up there at the moment, because he didn't say anything else.

"But why Bimbo, then?"

"Think back a few weeks."

Brenner preferred to keep mum, though.

"I can't permit myself to tell you even half of what I know. You know who Stenzl was, though, the man who got shot right before Bimbo's eyes."

"The boss at the blood bank."

"And the brother of Pro Med's chief."

How am I supposed to know that, Brenner thought. The murder of Stenzl and his girlfriend two weeks ago interested him about as much as any other story in the newspaper. He only caught what Bimbo and Munz had played up afterward. How Bimbo had managed to entangle himself in the nurses' rooms of every hospital ward, like he was some kind of Hollywood celebrity.

"Yeah, sure," Brenner said.

"What you don't know, though, is about the problems that Pro Med's been having with the blood bank. How Pro Med's Stenzl forced his own brother out of the company, but then didn't count on him taking over the blood bank."

Brenner didn't say anything.

"You know that Bimbo was the key witness, though. So you can put two and two together."

"Did you help get his brother installed at the blood bank after he got squeezed out of Pro Med?"

Once when he was in the fourth grade at Puntigam Elementary School, Brenner was rocking back and forth in his chair when it slipped right out from under him, and he hit the back of his head so hard on the desk behind him that he was unconscious for five minutes.

And he'd never forget the worried look on his teacher's face when he came to. Needless to say, big surprise now that, thirty-seven years later, he'd see that same worried look again.

"Things just aren't the same anymore in this city," Junior said, "since Pro Med brought politics into play. A single EMS organization can't survive in this city on donors alone. And two organizations—the city can't handle it. So politics comes into play."

"Pro Med does have its sponsors, though. You hardly see a Pro Med vehicle without the Watzek Concrete logo on it."

"I know, and the terminally ill believe they're getting picked up by a concrete mixer instead of an ambulance."

"That's the privatized economy for you. It's got its own laws."

"Privatized economy, don't make me laugh! I'll give you three guesses as to how Watzek is getting so many public construction contracts right now."

Brenner shrugged his shoulders: "That's how it goes when you've got ideals."

"Despite all their political ties, though, Pro Med has been unable to overtake us. Even though Stenzl has better contacts at City Hall." And then Junior said quietly: "Now he's turning to other means."

"You really believe that Pro Med had something to do with the murders?"

"The difference between believing and knowing is vast, Brenner. Exactly as vast as the difference between yesterday and today. Yesterday I had two reliable, experienced paramedics. And today, one of them's dead and the other's in prison. And yet, I should be glad that the matter got cleared up so quickly. Because this way the story will disappear from the newspapers within a few days."

"In that case, we're lucky that the newspapers haven't exploited it that drastically. At least, up until now."

"'Lucky,'" Junior said, reading off the ceiling. "'Lucky.' You could call it luck, I suppose. At least now I'll know why all these years I've been placing stock in the right type of cooperation with the newspapers. Why I put up with all the criticism internally here for allowing the newspapers to unofficially tap our radio. You know how it looks if the press photographer's already snapped a photo of the injured before we're even there on the scene. But today I feel validated by how crucial it's been for us to have a cooperative relationship with the media."

"I didn't know that the press taps our radio."

A thin smile crept out from under Junior's mustache. One of those smiles that makes the smilee out to be a naïve idiot.

"Have you never considered how the newspapers get their photos? They're not just tapping us. They're tapping the fire department radio and the police radio, too."

Junior acted as if he didn't notice Brenner's annoyance. To tell you the truth, though, I would've been annoyed, too, if somebody had approached me, asked if I could find out whether Pro Med taps our radio, and then later tells me that half the city's been listening in this whole time.

"If every hack reporter can tap our radio, then it can't be all that difficult for Pro Med, either."

This time Junior didn't read the answer off the ceiling.

Rather, you'd have thought it was written right on the pupils of Brenner's eyes. Junior leaned forward and then, in the way that you might talk to a silly child, he said: "When there's an unofficial agreement in place, it hardly takes a genius to tap a radio. The press knows our encryption code. But I'd rather be skinned alive before I betray our code to Pro Med."

"If every hack reporter knows the code, then Pro Med could've got it from them. They're not exactly the most discreet people. Given that they make it their job to broadcast total claptrap to the world."

"We're facing a scandal in the press. We've lost two of our most valuable employees. And Pro Med's lighting a fire under our asses like crazy. If it keeps on like this, in a couple months we'll be number two in EMS. And that means we'll be getting less money from the city and the state. And that means fewer vehicles and fewer drivers. It's like a chain reaction, and after a year, we'll only be half as big as Pro Med. And after another year, we'll be closing down. So you can find yourself a new job, Brenner. And don't give me any lectures. Bring me the proof once and for all that Pro Med's tapping our radio! And bring everything else that you learn about those Pro Meddlers to me, too! The more, the better! We've got to deliver the proof to the police about the kind of rotten organization Pro Med is, so that it becomes obvious who's behind the murders. And don't bungle things up this time—I don't want another one of my men to have to pay for it with his life!"

"That last part you're going to have to explain to me."

"Why do you think Bimbo was killed on the very day when you were phoning around half the city about how

Pro Med was tapping our radio? Very discreet, I have to say. I wouldn't have thought that you could manage all that by yourself."

You see: Free phone calls is one thing. The possibility of the dispatch center listening in is another thing altogether.

"You don't seriously think that Bimbo was killed because I—"

"All I know is that he was killed. A few hours, as a matter of fact, after you went around asking half the city how you could figure out whether Pro Med is tapping our radio. So, do me a favor, and going forward, use a little more discretion."

At the word "discretion" Junior banged his fist on the desk, not hard, because, glass top on the desk, but nevertheless, very uncomfortable for the ears when his bracelet struck the glass.

Brenner got up to leave, but before he reached the door, Junior said: "And you can forget about Angelika and her problems. Lanz has to stay right where he is for now. Until the whole thing gets cleared up. I don't want to see another person die. You and your overzealousness have already done enough."

Outside in the hall, it hit Brenner: the last time someone had talked to him like this. The last person who'd given him a half-hour lecture and who'd had the gall at the end to say: Don't give me any lectures.

He'd been on the force nineteen years at the time. He punched a hole through his hat from one day to the next simply because he couldn't get used to his new boss's style. This was a good two years ago. And now here we are again.

The way that Junior had no qualms about saddling him with the blame for Bimbo's death. Just like Nemec had done back then.

Now, you're going to say, You shouldn't always be looking back on life. Not the same old stories, that won't do you any good. But all I can say is this: if Junior hadn't reminded Brenner so much of Nemec at that moment, maybe the whole story would've turned out differently. Maybe he really would've accomplished everything with the radio and even done it fast just so he could finally be left alone again. And maybe today, we still wouldn't know how Bimbo's gold got in his throat.

And one more maybe:

Maybe, if after his conversation with Junior, Brenner hadn't been immediately dispatched on an über-Scheisshäusltour to Vienna General, who knows, maybe he never would've solved the case.

But, needless to say, when you're already at Vienna General, why not look in on Rosi for a spell?

"Liver transplant?" Rosi asked.

"Well, when you put it that way."

"That's clever," Rosi smirked. She wasn't particularly tall, but her trailer-converted-into-a-kitchen was so low that she always had to stoop a little while standing. And she was quite fat. And she had a lot of mustard and ketchup stains on her white surgeon's smock. And she had this fiery-red wavy hair that absorbed so much sweat from standing over a hot grill that it stuck out like horns from her head. "Sour mustard because you're sweet?"

"Did you go to the cemetery today or something?"

"Now why would I do a thing like that?"

"Where else would you dig up that old smarm?"

"Don't get fresh with me, young man!" Rosi smirked and popped a liver transplant right out in front of him.

"Young man? You could be my daughter."

"Nuh-uh! For that I'd have to shell out a ton on cosmetic surgery."

Brenner was glad to have his Leberkäse to turn to. And only after he took a couple of bites did he say: "Now, the way I reckon it, it's been all of two weeks since you shot Leo Stenzl."

"Yeah, and you better watch out, because today I've got an itch in my finger again."

"As long as it's just your finger."

Another bite of Leberkäse now, and then: "Only thing saving you's the fact that you've got no window on the music-pavilion side. Otherwise, you'd be a prime suspect."

"It hasn't got to the point that I need a window on that side yet. Not until I don't know where to put the chocolate bars and the Neapolitan wafers anymore."

"So you didn't see anything."

"I saw something, alright. I was counting my money just then. And that's what I saw."

"Why wasn't Lanz in the photo in the newspaper? Just Bimbo and Munz?"

"Lanz wasn't even here. Bimbo got it all wrong. Lanz only pulled in as fast as he did because he was actually coming from the airport with a donor kidney just then. I still have to laugh about him. Because he was up at surgery like lightning."

"Like lightning. And then it thundered."

"Exactly. Then it thundered. But not for Lanz—for Stenzl," Rosi had to laugh again.

"What did Stenzl actually do?"

"Nothing. He was a real desk jockey."

Brenner hadn't meant Stenzl's job, because that was the one and only thing he did know. So he tried it a different way: "Let me guess, more jockey than desk, though, right?"

"You can say that again."

"But nobody used it against him?"

"Why use something like that against him when you've got a perfectly good bullet?" Rosi grinned. "Besides, how should I know? You're the one who should know better."

"Why me?"

"Your organization makes its living off blood donors. So you must've known Stenzl."

"My organization?"

"You and your whole Pro Med."

That was Rosi's favorite joke. As a matter of principle, she called the Pro Meddlers Rapid Responders and the Rapid Responders Pro Meddlers. Just like she called the Brothers of Mercy the Sisters of Charity and vice versa.

In this case, though, it really didn't make a difference for once. Because Pro Med Vienna makes its living off blood donors and Vienna Rapid Response makes its living off blood donors. And so did Leo Stenzl. Only, he wasn't living anymore.

CHAPTER 7

"Maybe I'll actually see some profits today," Rosi said, surprised. "Those two from the detective squad were back again."

"And? Whose sports coat did you like better?"

"The boss's."

"How could you tell which one was the boss?"

"He didn't eat anything."

"They're always thinking about their cholesterol, those leadership types," Brenner said, before shoveling another bite of Leberkäse into his mouth.

"Sindelka's different. He already came by today, too."

"Sindelka from Autopsy?"

"No, Sindelka from the state-certified virgins." Because Rosi was one of those people who couldn't give a straight yes.

"He usually doesn't come by until the afternoon. Him and his heart transplant, day in and day out, and still as skinny as a pencil."

"Maybe he's really into sports."

"Nuh-uh! His only sport's carving up corpses."

"So that's why."

"That's why what?"

"Why he doesn't ever gain any weight. Cadaverine," Brenner said, gravely.

"Nuh-uh!"

Brenner used his last bite of bread to wipe up some mustard while Rosi continued: "He even had to cut Stenzl and Irmi apart."

"What do you mean, 'cut them apart'?"

"I mean cut them apart," Rosi explained. "Because first the bullet went through his tongue and then it went through hers. And the heat from the bullet melted their two tongues together."

"Nuh-uh!"

"Really!" Rosi shot back. "Do you think Sindelka is lying to me?"

"That's some job he's got," Brenner said, his own career situation suddenly appearing to him in a somewhat rosier light.

"Terrible," Rosi said, making a face and cutting a ten-pack of Weisswurst out of its foil. "A tongue like that must be grisly. Have you ever had beef tongue before?"

"Of course."

"Me, too. Once—and once was enough! It comes with a layer of Letscho served over it so that you can't really see the tongue. The nubs and all. But I ate the goulash layer first."

"That was a mistake."

"You can say that again. Because then you see the cow's tongue lying there on your plate. The shape and the nubs and everything."

"That's not good."

"And then, while you're eating it, all the sudden you

realize that you've got a tongue on top of your tongue. Terrible, I tell you. You don't know anymore if the cow's sucking on your tongue or you're sucking on its."

"But something like that wouldn't bother Sindelka."

"Nothing bothers him at all. That kind of thing's right up his alley!"

"That's the feeling I get, too."

"Do you know what he said about Irmi and Stenzl's tongues being melted together?" Rosi said, grinning.

"What would I know?"

"That at least they're joined for life."

"He's right, if you look at it that way."

"It was getting to the point that Nicole started to get jealous."

"And who might Nicole be?"

"Stenzl's secretary over at the blood bank. She and Irmi were at each other's throats over Stenzl, and I'm not kidding—the claws came out."

Nuh-uh, Brenner thought.

And then crossed the street and walked right into the blood bank.

When he walked in, he thought he was in the wrong place at first. Even though he'd been in there countless times before, because needless to say, distributing packaged blood to the hospitals is one of the main *Scheisshäusltouren* that EMTs loathe doing. But usually Brenner was always there in the mornings, when the place was teeming with EMTs and nurses lined up to get the blood. And now, completely deserted.

The dispensing window for the blood didn't look much

different than the baggage window at the train station, where they were always shooing the bums out of the storage lockers. Except that here, there wasn't a train employee sitting behind the window. Instead, a young woman was lying motionless on the floor. And believe it or not, the first thing Brenner noticed is how pretty her long brown hair looked as it fell on the parquet floor all around her head. And only as a second item of business did he notice how her white lab coat had slid up to her hips.

And I wonder how come everybody in the hospital has always got those white coats on. Even Rosi's always got one on, with mustard and ketchup stains all over it. At least in her case, you can say she needs it. But what's a secretary at the blood bank need a lab coat for? The blood packs are completely sealed and sterilized—not like at Rosi's. Or maybe it's just a practical matter at a hospital so you can tell the staff apart from the patients. You see, that must be the reason right there.

"Ever hear of knocking?" the dead woman asked Brenner, but still without moving a muscle, expect for her mouth, of course.

"I did knock."

She opened her eyes and, in all honesty, I've got to say—though I've never looked a Martian in the eyes, this is roughly how I'd imagine it. And not what you're thinking, green—no, brown. It was the shape, though, a rather unnatural slant to the pupils that'd make you think Martian eyes, i.e. mesmerizing.

"Sometimes when I'm doing my stretches, I feel so relaxed that I don't even hear anyone knocking."

"So that's what they call sleeping on the job these days: stretching."

"What a load of papperlapapp—sleeping on the job," and as she said so, she rolled onto her side in one effortless movement. "Do you know what the most important thing is? You can't ever go from lying flat on your back to standing up. Always roll onto your side first."

Then she stood up with such intent that you'd have thought there was some kind of religious practice going on, Buddhism or somesuch where they can't eat cows, and it used to be that we made fun of them for it, but now, mad cow disease, and they're the ones laughing at us.

It even seemed to Brenner like her hair fell over her back in slow motion. And I have to say, maybe that was the reason she had a lab coat on. Her brown hair supplied such a pleasing contrast, such bounce and body to it, when just moments earlier on the parquet floor, Brenner had been thinking it was the hair of a dead woman.

Then she finally smoothed down her lab coat, sat down on her swivel chair, and with a highly official blink of the eyes, said: "How can I be of service?"

"I've been dispatched to help with today's stretches."

"Very funny."

"So, I'm always getting these terrible headaches, you know. Migraines. And the doctor said they're from muscle cramps in my neck. And only stretching will help. Unfortunately the insurance won't cover it. But then I got some advice: go to the blood bank, there are stretches to be had—under the counter."

"Very, very funny."

You're going to say, a little pushy, the way Brenner's talking, a bit much, like the way men used to talk. But I'm only going to tell you once. Here it is: people connect by talking. And by saying "very funny" a few times, already it's turned out that the secretary really does do her stretches for her own headaches. And after the two suits pestered her again with questions today—for the third time now in two weeks—well, she really needed those stretches.

And for her part, she could gather that Brenner really was the foremost expert in headaches. "But do you know what the good thing about headaches is, Nicole?" he asked.

She looked at him, stunned, as if her and her brown eyes had never been called by her own name before. But did she say anything out loud? No.

"At least you know that you've still got a head."

"Very funny."

"Because if you put a bullet in someone's head, they won't ever have the chance of getting a headache."

"But I don't put bullets in people's heads."

"But somehow a bullet got put in your boss's head."

"Watch what you say. He may have been a bad boss, a lazy dog who had me doing all his work, but I wouldn't have shot him for it."

"Maybe not because he was a bad boss. Maybe you shot him because of what a bad lover he was."

Brenner! I'm compelled to criticize him some. Earlier with Rosi, maybe he'd just been teasing her when he suggested she'd shot Stenzl. But the fun stops here. And Nicole's eyes can only serve as a partial excuse. I can only explain this type of sink-or-swim method of Brenner's on account of the fire that Junior had lit under his ass. And with a fire under your ass, you tend to take a certain plunge.

He saw Nicole dial her eyelids up to level three, and she'd just managed to wipe the moist film from her eyes when something occurred to him now: A trick: say something nice.

"So does the stretching actually do anything for headaches?" he asked with a smile.

First something nice, and then something interesting: "I haven't had any more headaches since I started working EMS."

And Nicole eyed him suspiciously: "That's usually when people start getting headaches."

Then Brenner showed her the packet of pills that Czerny had sold him. Because Czerny, with his head for business, also happened to carry on some modest drug dealing. And I don't want to go around blabbing too much now, it's really no big deal, but thanks to his access to doctors, he'd amassed a small arsenal of drug samples and was selling them to his circle of friends and associates. Just an on-the-side thing and nothing more.

"Every day before breakfast, and ever since, no headaches."

Only now did the tears vanish from those Martian eyes for good. Brenner could tell that for a fact when she batted them open to look at the packet he was showing her.

Then she left the room, and came back a few minutes later with a giant red folder, from which she read the side effects to Brenner.

"How long have you been on them?"

"Three, four months."

"Then you should be glad they haven't taken you to the hazardous-waste station by now," she howled. "If I were you, I'd check myself into the Intensive Care Unit pronto. Let me have that poison right now!" Her eyes were as narrow as the slot in the disposal box for expired meds.

Brenner handed the pills over without objection, because at home he had hundreds. Not just hundreds of pills, but hundreds of packets.

"I don't understand why EMTs are at such risk of addiction," Nicole said, shaking her head. "I'm sure you got this poison from Czerny."

"And I'm sure you know that from Stenzl," Brenner said, imitating her girly singsong voice.

"Papperlapapp! Everybody knows about Czerny and his pill services, that greedy jackal. If I were the cops I'd have him under the magnifying glass in no time. Because he's got no scruples. And besides, he's the only one who profits from Stenzl's death."

"Because he takes over Stenzl's job and goes from small-time to big-time?"

"Papperlapapp! A lot of bad things can be said about Leo. But this pill business of Czerny's was the one thing he never had anything to do with."

"But he was doing business with Czerny?"

"Czerny can talk a deal up to anybody, and you can bet he'll always be the one who comes out ahead. He's got life insurance deals going with every other hospital employee that are based on matching funds. Of course, Czerny's never the one that dies, though. It's the others that die, of course.

"And he had a deal like that with Stenzl?"

"That's what I'm trying to say."

"But how can he afford something like that? Insurance ain't cheap."

"What do you mean, 'afford'? He pushes policies for the insurance company, and his commission nets him back half of what he put in. Allegedly he's got over a hundred active policies. Each one for over a million at least."

"And statistically, at least one person out of a hundred is going to die each year," Brenner calculated.

"Spare me your statistics."

"Otherwise there'd be people over a hundred years old."

"If you look at it like that, sure."

"Of course you've got to factor in the age pyramid, though. And balancing the premium payments with the mortality rate, it gets complicated. The insurance companies aren't stupid, either."

"No they're not. But people are. Czerny's already worked it all out with the insurance."

"You mean the balancing part?"

"If it so happens that in a given year the balance is off and nobody dies, then you've just got to give them a little nudge," Nicole said. And then suddenly she smiled. "I'm just talking nonsense. I hope you don't take it too seriously!"

"Seeing as they shot your boyfriend a few weeks ago, you're in an awfully good mood."

"Who says so?"

"I do. Or do you see somebody else here?"

"Who's calling him my boyfriend?"

"Everybody is."

Brenner took a step back just to be on the safe side. But Nicole didn't try to take a lunge at him. She just asked in an icy Martian tone: "What is it that everybody's saying?"

"That you and Irmi were at each other's throats."

"Well, that's true. But it doesn't mean for a second that I was interested in Stenzl. I wanted Irmi out of here because she was always snooping around. There was something off about her."

"And there was nothing between you and Stenzl?"

"No, thank you very much."

How are you supposed to tell if someone is telling the truth with eyes like that? So now Brenner just said: "Well, if you didn't shoot him, then it must've been Czerny."

"Very funny. I admit I don't like Czerny with all his wheeling and dealing. But that whole thing with the insurance is really nothing more than a game of roulette. He puts his money on different people and hopes that one of them will die on time."

"I hope it's not Russian roulette."

"It's not all that different than you and your fellow EMTs, gambling away your paychecks. Your organization plays down at the Kellerstüberl," Nicole said, acting the stern nurse again, "and the Pro Meddlers play at the Golden Heart. It's the same everywhere. Doesn't surprise me one bit about Lanz and Bimbo."

"And how do you know about that again?"

"Why do you think the detectives were here today?"

"Maybe they like you?"

"Did I hear a *maybe*?"

"And you weren't surprised at all?"

"That the police like me?"

"That Lanz killed Bimbo."

"Truthfully, no. Not with what Lanz owed Bimbo from gambling."

"Sounds like you know all about that, too."

She kept her head perfectly still and shot him a punishing look for a few seconds. Which gave Brenner a chance to notice her faint Hansi-Munz mustache. Believe it or not, though, it somehow made her all the prettier.

"Everybody knows about the gambling debts you guys have racked up. The Pro Meddlers are no better, though. You wouldn't believe how much they play for at the Golden Heart."

"You frequent the Golden Heart?" Brenner asked.

"I used to."

"How come only used to?"

"Back before Stenzl became my boss. He owned the place. Or at least half of it."

"And who did the other half belong to?"

"How should I know? His brother, I think. But then, when Stenzl became my boss six months ago, I would've felt weird going there after work, too. Especially since he and his brother were on the outs."

"Did you tell the police that part, too?"

"You think I'm going to escort those carbon copy cops to the Golden Heart?"

Brenner wondered if that was an invitation. But caution made him say something else: "Carbon copy cops! That's a good one. And yet, you can still tell right away who's the boss."

"Obviously. The one who smells like sweat."

Women and their sense of smell, Brenner thought, but he left it at that. He still had that invitation to get back to: "But now you can go to the Golden Heart again?"

"As a matter of fact, I could go right now."

"How about tonight at ten?"

"But you'll be the first of your kind to risk going there. Into enemy territory."

"But, with you, I won't be afraid."

"Papperlapapp!"

"So, ten o'clock?"

"On one condition: you hand over the pills you've got back at home."

Brenner felt a little dumb now on account of how Nicole had seen right through him with her X-ray eyes.

"I know the kind of rabble I'm dealing with," she said with a smile.

And it was this smile that kept Brenner preoccupied until ten o'clock, much more so than the question of who killed Bimbo and Stenzl.

The next day, though, Brenner didn't know if his headache was from not taking the pills or just because he'd been boozing it up at the Golden Heart until four o'clock in the morning with Nicole.

Or if it was from processing the fact that the bartender at the Golden Heart was, of all people, Angelika Lanz.

CHAPTER 8

His head felt as if a throbbing new shoot had sprouted from it overnight. It was only when he saw his bloodshot eye in the mirror that it started to come back to him. A fragmentary recap as he touched the fragmented skin on his cheek.

Although, Brenner had always had red, pockmarked skin. And centimeter-deep vertical ruts in his cheeks, as if he was hiding a pair of razor blades in them. Today, though, the whole left half of his face was peeling off like a poorly shellacked mannequin. And his left ear, completely deaf.

Of course, you could also say that the ass-kicking he got at four o'clock in the morning didn't necessarily have to be the reason for his migraine. A migraine-brain like Brenner's is just unpredictable. Sometimes you get an attack for no reason at all. And other times you get a kick to the head, and you feel marvelous, like an old TV that just needs a good old smack now and then.

But Brenner's head was hurting way too much to be matching up cause and effect now. He was standing in front of the mirror and thinking: Unbelievable that Nicole could drop him like a block of cement.

But as he washed the blood off his face and watched it

run down the drain, a few more details came back to him. And as he toweled off, he realized that it hadn't been Nicole who'd knocked him around with a cement club.

And as he got dressed, he remembered precisely how, at four in the morning, he and Nicole left the Golden Heart. And how they didn't get very far. Not because that's how drunk they were. But because two men got out of a truck and told Nicole to scram.

Now he remembered all over again how the one guy asked him if he was Brenner, and before he could even nod his head, the other guy was launching into him in a way that made Brenner's whole body nod.

As he looked at his mangled uniform, it came back to him how the two guys had mopped the pavement with him outside the Golden Heart. Maybe I shouldn't have gone to the Pro Meddler's bar in my uniform, Brenner reconsidered now. And immediately his head punished him. Because thinking, always bad for a headache.

Not-thinking, though, even worse, because then, pure headache's all you've got in your skull. So now Brenner thinks: I could call in sick. But then the next thought: calling in sick at the last second, not exactly highly regarded by his colleagues. Somebody would've said: We present you with the Collegiality Cup because we're so grateful to you for calling in sick at the last minute.

It's not like at an office where the work'll still be there waiting for you the next day: the accident victims, the heart attacks, they expect nothing less than same-day delivery— even the suicides get a little fidgety if you don't cut them down right away. Don't get sore at me, that's how the EMTs talk amongst themselves. It's not meant in bad taste, but more like a defensive mechanism.

Brenner had two possibilities now. Either I call in sick. Or I don't call in sick.

And these days, when you're in headache mode and you're faced with two possibilities, it's the pits. So Brenner decides to just stumble down to the courtyard so that at least the possibilities will ease up on him.

Impossible he could've driven, though. Because he was half-blind from his migraine. Unless you count yourself among the foremost migraine experts, you can't know all about that. There are people who think they're having a migraine just because they get a sharp little twinge at their temples. But these are the same people who confuse a toenail-clipping with foot amputation.

In the crew room, Brenner noticed that the new schedule had been posted. Needless to say now, hope. Maybe he had the day off today.

On the contrary, though. He was on today, tomorrow, and the next three and a half weeks, according to fat Nuttinger's new punishment plan. Twelve hours a day for three and a half weeks straight without a single day off.

And when he saw that, and when he noticed his co-workers' snide grins all around, it came back to him. All of it. It all came flooding back. And you see, a person could certainly come up with some theories, i.e. migraine psychology. That maybe the Brenner-brain had only hatched a migraine so that he wouldn't have to remember.

But one look at the monthly schedule and the snide grins all around and the whole migraine was of no use—he would have to remember it now after all. How in his stupor last night, he got his ass kicked so bad, it'd left him lying on the sidewalk. And how someone must've called for an ambulance.

Because why else would a Pro Med vehicle have been seen just minutes later driving into the Rapid Response yard for the first time since the Battle of Solferino? Where, startled, all the volunteers went streaming out into the courtyard at four in the morning. Because, just then, the triumphant Pro Meddlers were unloading the dazed Rapid Responder in his shredded uniform.

It was all coming back to Brenner now. And for the first time in his life he was glad for the migraines, because they did in fact drape a certain veil over life.

When you're in this condition, nothing else matters to you. You don't care if the person next to you is whistling, or if the guy across from you is talking in that grating tone of his, or if somebody in that guy's vicinity is breathing, or if somebody's jangling their eyelashes so much that it nearly ruptures your eardrum. You don't even care if you've brought disgrace on yourself, or if you've been scheduled, punitively speaking, to three and a half weeks straight of work.

Two minutes later, Brenner was already hotfooting it to the vehicle. A heart attack. Lights and sirens. Brenner was barely out of hearing range of the station before he turned the sirens off. But his two heads, both, got such a thrill out of the *wheeeeoooo-wheeeeoooo* that they picked up where the sirens had left off and just kept blaring it out at him.

His one and only stroke of luck was that his partner today was the quiet 8K. Because, besieged by the chatter of a Czerny or a Hansi Munz, he definitely wouldn't have survived the day.

And the patient they'd landed in the ninth district didn't do any talking on the drive either. He had a lovely antiques store on Porzellangasse. Today, though, he was the one showing signs of aging. Because, middle of broad daylight in his own antiques store, he collapses.

He was lying on the gray linoleum floor, white as chalk, and staring at Brenner, scared out of his wits—and silent. And unbelievable luck for Brenner: the young shopgirl didn't utter a word, either, out of fright. She hung a note on the door anyhow, though: "TEMPORARILY CLOSED DUE TO ILLNESS."

And you see, the second you're not watching—employees already wasting paper! Because if she'd waited ten minutes, she could've just written: "CLOSED DUE TO DEATH OF OWNER."

Brenner and the quiet 8K tried to resuscitate him, but it was hopeless. Don't go thinking that it was Brenner's fault, now. A heart massage is strenuous goddamn work, even if you're in good shape. You'll have sweat streaming down you, boy, even if you're at it for just a few minutes. But, today of all days, it actually did Brenner some good.

Because you've got to kneel over the dying person with arms outstretched like so, and then the rhythmic movements. Somehow it almost gave Brenner a reciprocal massage today. The way the dying man's chest pressed back so nice and rhythmically against Brenner's arms, it practically rippled out, massage-like, to his petrified neck muscles. Well, don't go thinking that his headache had gone away, but maybe some momentary alleviation. Maybe a little like those exercises of Nicole's.

The fact that the man then died was just so typical of how this whole day was going. Because it's just as often that somebody doesn't die on you. Far outnumbered by the rides where nothing dramatic happens. A broken leg to urgent care. A kid with scarlet fever to the isolation unit. Parkinson's to physical therapy. A cancer patient to radiation.

I don't want to get carried away here—I don't know if you know this or not, but when I get started on the topic of disease, I can actually feel my organs itching me. Brenner, though, during those weeks when he was on fat Nuttinger's punishment plan of zero days off, needless to say, he had to see quite a bit.

On Day Two he got paired up with the shop boss. Who had to jump in and cover for Lanz for the time being, even though he himself had more than enough to do back in the vehicle repair shop.

"If I'm filling in the driver gap, we're just going to end up with a vehicle gap," he grumbled. "There's just not enough of us to go around." Because the 590 with the broken tailpipe— the one where the patient was almost asphyxiated a few weeks ago—still not repaired.

The next day, Brenner's blue eye gradually turned green, and he got paired up with Hansi Munz. When they got a call for a suicide, Hansi Munz cut down the hanged, and with the next of kin right there next to him, he says to Brenner: "Hemp allergy."

It seemed to Brenner that with each passing day Hansi Munz was getting more and more like Bimbo, as if in

Hansi Munz, the spirit of Bimbo now—spirit donor, so to speak.

The day after that, Brenner got paired up with an 8K, then two days with Czerny, then back with Hansi Munz again, and then, on the day where he noticed his green eye was now starting to turn yellow, he got paired up with Nechvatel who listened to nothing but Zillertaler-Schürzenjäger cassettes the whole time. Then, two days with an 8K, and by then, his days and his partners and his hematoma slowly began to blur together.

And it's a peculiar effect, true for most people, Brenner was no exception. You fear nothing more than your life consisting only of work, that all you're doing is running like a hamster on its wheel. But then, when you truly are overworked, when there's no chance of you getting off the wheel, something in the brain must change. It must be like with marathon runners, who produce a certain substance that makes running suddenly very easy for them.

Somehow Brenner enjoyed it, how the work kept him from ever having to think anymore. Just like with marathon runners, too, or managers, let's say, they enjoy not having to think as long as they keep producing this substance.

Brenner drove and drove and drove. Two or three hundred kilometers every day in city traffic. And if on average a call takes seven or eight kilometers, then, that's—wait—or let's say, for simplicity's sake, it takes ten kilometers. Then, that's twenty to thirty calls a day! Twenty to thirty times a day of putting a sick person on a stretcher, encouraging him, distracting him from his suffering a little.

Because, out of twenty or thirty runs, at most, every tenth

one is an emergency. At most. That's two or three times a day that you find yourself having to reason: If I go against orders and run the red light, maybe the injured person will survive, and then his three kids will still have a father, and they'll be allowed to go to school and study and the boy will become a gym teacher and the girl a tax consultant, and the youngest, smart as a whip, she'll graduate with honors, finish school in record time, and then, head physician down in Mexico.

But only if I charge through the red. Only if I nearly graze a pedestrian. But if I sit and wait for that last bit of red to drain out of the light, then he could possibly bleed to death on me and then, needless to say, financial problems for the family. And then, you can nix college, of course. And while you're at it, you can nix the head physician in Mexico, too, more like head waitress at La Cantina Mexicana.

Decisions like these, though, rare. And otherwise, it's a little caregiving, a little encouragement. And most of the time, not even that. Mostly just listening to old people. Or just acting like you're listening to them. Because they're not seeking consolation. They just want to recite their same damn story for the hundred-thousandth time.

And when you look at it that way, being an EMT is an interesting profession. Because you learn something about people. You listen to the old folks' stories, and they tell you every detail of their most personal ailment a hundred times. As though life devises a unique malady for each person. Because they don't know what you, as an EMT, figured out after just a couple weeks on the job: that down to the last hair, it's the same damn story.

The patients' stories, though, those are still bearable, compared to your co-workers' stories. Because co-worker stories, always insufferable, i.e. mortgage contract, i.e. tutor for their dim kid, i.e. marital matters. Brenner couldn't even begin to comprehend it—the stuff of marital intimacy getting dished out to you in minute detail. But every day it bothered him less. And by the eleventh or twelfth day, he didn't really register it at all anymore. The marathon substance had a completely neutralizing effect on his co-workers' stories.

Too much substance can be dangerous, too, though. Because Brenner was starting to get a little childish when he began imitating the voices that came in over the radio all day long. Especially Hansi Munz's quacker of a voice— with each passing day, Brenner was able to pull it off better. And there were moments where he whined along with the patients à la Hansi Munz. It crossed into the danger zone, though, when at the start of his third week, he nearly didn't hear who beat him up out in front of the Golden Heart.

"Last week I was on vacation," Lil' Berti told him.

For god's sake. Must produce substance now. Always going on about their vacations, people. You can hardly hold it against Brenner.

"You do know it's stuck with me, the idea of the detective agency."

For Christ's sake. Lil' Berti, always going on about his detective agency. On the other hand, though, out of all of them, he truly was the nicest one. By now, Brenner was managing not to listen, thanks to the substance, and yet, in spite of it, he could converse a little with Lil' Berti: "Were you on the beach when you started making plans for your detective agency?"

"No, no, I didn't leave town."

"That's right."

"Travel doesn't do much for me."

"Don't I know it."

"These days even the garbage travels."

"You can say that again."

"In fact, I always say, it's only the garbage that travels these days," Berti laughed.

"Only the garbage, that's a good one."

"Not to mention with a job like ours. Where every day we're driving three hundred kilometers."

That's it, Berti, Brenner thought. And in his thoughts he was someplace else altogether, boarding his thought-jet, as it were. And while we're on the topic, I've got to say: traveling these days, often viewed critically. Because mass tourism and all that, and people trotting all over the globe and becoming more and more narrow-minded in spite of it. The thought-jet deserves a critical look, too, though. Because while you're thought-jetting off somewhere, maybe somebody back home's trying to tell you how it came to pass that you got a crash course in the cement business, so to speak, three weeks ago.

Interesting parallel, though! Just like when you travel-travel through different countries and notice how people just get more and more similar, the same thing happens along the flight path of a thought-jet, too, where even in the farthest-flung destinations, who do you run into? Nobody but old acquaintances and the folks from back home. You know how people often say the world's a village? Well, the thought-world's just a village, too.

And just as Berti was telling him: "I've been here nearly three years now, first as an Eight-K and now staff. But you know what, it's a detective agency that I find really appealing," thought-wise, Brenner was already with old Frau Rupprechter, the diabetic who they were on their way to pick up from the hospital just then.

Every day she got delivered to the hospital and every day she got picked back up again. Banker's widow, she's got the insurance, don't even ask. And on top of that, she's already donated two ambulances. And if Frau Rupprechter thought it'd be a lark to lug her Döblinger villa on a trailer behind the ambulance day after day, why, they would've arranged that, too.

Brenner went to pick her up from internal medicine, while Berti waited in the vehicle. Interesting, though: in reality, she was a few years older than she was on Brenner's thought-jet. And the skin on her cheeks, a little thinner. And her wrath, a little more biblical.

"Next time why don't you just let me spend the night here!" she said, hollering at Brenner and beating her cane on the cement floor. Even though Brenner had arrived five minutes early like he always did for Her Rupprechtress.

It didn't put him out any, though, because of the marathon substance. And then, as she launched into her endless litany about the ninnies on the nursing staff, Brenner simply booked a return flight on his thought-jet, back over to Berti, where he could now listen to what Berti had told him a few minutes ago, practically a mental VCR.

"At the start of the VISTAA program, we all had a basic training together. There were thirty-eight of us at the time. A few then went on to the fire department, a few to the nursing home, a few to the state government, and so on. A guy I got along with pretty good ended up over at Pro Med. Well, last week I call him up to see whether I might tempt him to open up a detective agency with me."

A staccato rapid-fire pierced through Brenner's thoughts. It was Frau Rupprechter's cane, which she was rapping on the floor like the needle of a sewing machine.

Because she could tell for a fact that Brenner wasn't paying attention. She was still yammering on about the incompetent nursing staff. And one really oughtn't speak ill of the dead, but that was no concern of Frau Rupprechter's. Because she was even laying into Irmi now, who'd been her home health care nurse for years. You'd have thought she was mad at Irmi for getting herself shot. Practically an imposition for the ninety-year-old Frau Rupprechter to have to get used to a new nurse now.

"A curious person," Frau Rupprechter griped.

"Yes, Frau Rupprechter."

"Sticking her nose all over the place."

"Yes, Frau Rupprechter."

"That nosy gal!"

"Yes, Frau Rupprechter."

You could tell from his monotonous replies that Brenner had already hit cruising altitude back on the other thought-jet. Berti and his detective agency were, at this moment, still better than Her Rupprechtress.

"So my pal at Pro Med says: he's not interested in

opening up a detective agency, but he'll be glad to help out. Well, I had last week off—basically a test to see if I've got what it takes, detective-wise. If, in one week, I can find out who beat you up out front of the Golden Heart."

You'd like to think that Frau Rupprechter and her endless litany wouldn't be interesting enough to make Brenner swerve back and forth from Lil' Berti to her.

But that's the old irony of travel. The far-flung always strikes you as more interesting even if, viewed from up close, it's completely uninteresting. Although I've got to say, a case of persecution mania like Frau Rupprechter's isn't actually all that uninteresting—just horribly irritating, but that's a whole 'nother subject altogether.

And one thing you can't forget. These days when you're severely diabetic, you're automatically half blind, too. That's the cow-blindness that comes from sugar, don't ask me how, I'm no optometrist.

"She thought I couldn't see how she was constantly rummaging around in my papers," Frau Rupprechter said, giving the woman—who'd been her in-home nurse for years—hell all the way to the grave.

"Didn't she have paperwork to take care of with you?" Brenner asked, playing the interested part a little, because Frau Rupprechter, always a generous tipper.

"Of course!" Rupprechter barked at Brenner. Because, after her treatments, Rupprechter was always a little more intolerant than usual, i.e. flip side of the coin she tipped you.

Brenner wasn't upset for long, though, because in his head, he was back with Berti.

"So my buddy asks around Pro Med a little. Well, it's

an open secret there that it was two truck drivers from the Watzek cement company that worked you over."

"Watzek's the one that's got their corporate logo on every other Pro Med vehicle."

Alas. This reply didn't occur to Brenner until just now, when he was finally getting Frau Rupprechter, who was only able to inch her feet forward, into the vehicle. And you see, that's why I always say, always respond right away if you can. Because as Brenner's opening the door now, he says:

"You should definitely open up a detective agency."

And only then did he lean into the cab and see that, in the meantime, Berti had disappeared into thin air.

CHAPTER 9

Brenner definitely wasn't the type to immediately fear the worst all the time. Quite the opposite, back when he was on the force, he even skipped a couple of assignments because, false alarm, he thought. And then it took him three times the effort to sweep the case under the rug.

So, when a person like this immediately fears the worst, needless to say, twice as alarming. He gave it five minutes before he couldn't stand waiting anymore, and then, he just let Frau Rupprechter sit up front with him. He drove over to Rosi's and asked her if she'd seen Lil' Berti.

"Go ask at the Laundromat," Rosi advised him. "They face out onto the parking lot there."

"Where's the Laundromat?"

"Over there where they've got the mirrored windows."

Brenner was still a little puzzled why the Laundromat of all places would have mirrored windows. When he went in, though, he got why. Leave it to Rosi to call a morgue a Laundromat.

Back in high school, Brenner once visited the Puntigam brewery on the day when it would annually open its doors to the public. Needless to say, free beer, and his first bout of intoxication was so horrendous that it was also his last. He was still shy at the time, though, and the visitors were all led into this enormous hall—big enough to hold a swimming pool. No pool, though, just a bathtub next to some other vats, because that's where the beer's stored until it's ready to drink. And as Brenner entered that refrigerated hall of beer, what was his first thought: This is just how I imagine a morgue to look.

And, for a fifteen-year-old, not a bad thought! Though everything here at the morgue was different in the details: only two bathtubs, and a refrigeration wall, and tables and gurneys with corpses on them, but the overall impression, quite similar nonetheless. And even the young technician in his lab coat now reminded Brenner of the Puntigam brewing engineer who'd led the tour back then.

He was no mere corpse-bather, though, no, he had a specialized task. Because at a hospital as huge as Vienna General, needless to say, a lot of amputated limbs, and they've got to be disposed of. The embryo goes into the skin cream, so it's got another use, but a smoker's leg, for instance, can't recycle that. And you can't just toss it into the garbage can, either.

"Hello, can I help you with something?" the young man asked, politely enough but without looking up, because he was struggling a little with a leg that was almost too long for the oven. "My colleagues are all on their lunch breaks right now."

Brenner was so surprised to find a smart young person working here that his purpose almost escaped him. "I'm looking for my co-worker."

The medical-waste technician jammed the oven door shut behind the leg and turned around to face Brenner: "He's not one of these?" he pointed at the five, six corpses that were lying out in the open.

"My co-worker's not dead," Brenner said. But he also must not have been completely certain at that moment, or else he wouldn't have cast a cautious glance at the corpses.

"Then you're in the wrong place," the boy said with a smile. He had such a perceptive face that Brenner thought: Probably either a student or a perv.

"You look out onto the parking lot from here," Brenner began. Because, on that account, Rosi was right, these were bona-fide panoramic views of the emergency vehicle lot.

"Not very often. It's more interesting here inside," he grinned.

Maybe not a student after all, Brenner reconsidered.

"Nevertheless, did you by any chance notice anything unusual outside there in the last half hour?"

"Something unusual in the emergency parking lot? You mean like an EMT without sunglasses or a mustache?"

"EMT, sunglasses, no mustache, nearly six and a half feet tall, and skinny as Mickey Mouse."

"That's your co-worker?"

"Exactly. And he gave me the slip outside there."

"I'm afraid I haven't noticed anyone matching that description. And I wouldn't have had the chance to, either. Namely, because there was a truck parked in front of that window for a long time."

"Since when do they let trucks park out there?"

"That's what I wondered, too," the boy said, and then his

oven beeped, roughly like how a microwave beeps, and he opened the door and stuffed the next leg in.

"Did the truck have a logo on it?"

"Didn't notice."

"Watzek, maybe?"

"No clue," the young man said, because he wasn't some yea-sayer—students and pervs generally aren't. Always chasing their intellectual autonomy or whatnot.

When Brenner got back to the vehicle, the first thing he saw was that the radio microphone had been torn out. "What did you do with the radio microphone, Frau Rupprechter?"

Believe it or not: Just because Brenner left her alone for five minutes, she tried to call for help over the radio. Needless to say, instead of pushing the one and only button on the microphone, though, in her impatience and wrath she thought it better to rip the whole cable out.

"As soon as I get home I'm filing a complaint about you," she said.

"Yes, Frau Rupprechter."

"Where's your colleague?"

"Dead, Frau Rupprechter."

But he was just saying that to scare her now. The thing is, he ended up scaring himself more than he did the old lady. By the time he was finally rid of her, Brenner needed to return to the station and pick up a new mic.

Back at the Response Center, nobody said anything about Lil' Berti, and Brenner didn't mention that he'd disappeared, either. He just hoped he'd get put on a halfway-decent call or two where he could look for Berti a little on the side. As the devil would have it, though, one emergency after another.

And then, that evening, a call that almost made him forget about Lil' Berti altogether.

The woman seemed familiar to him right away. Even though age had changed her, of course. And the cancer had changed her even more. As for all the things that'd changed Brenner, well, he preferred not to know.

Nevertheless, the two recognized each other almost simultaneously. Not right away, though. First, the timid look away, and then another sniff, and then a look away again, and then a bit of a smile, and then simultaneously:

"Is it you—?" and then embarrassed laughter, even though they'd once sworn eternal love back in high school in Puntigam.

"Klara!" Brenner said, grinning.

And Klara arched her eyebrows in the exact same affected manner that had always impressed Brenner back then.

Just so his instincts wouldn't take over all the sudden, you know, from all the grinning and eyebrow-arching, he quickly added: "So you ended up in Vienna, too."

"Twenty-eight years ago."

Twenty-eight years ago, you were just a kindergartner back in Puntigam. Or: You must've just been a bun in the oven. Or: Did you get left behind on a high school field trip? Or whatever else a person might say in a situation like this.

Maybe best not to make any jokes about age, though, to a person who's on their way to chemo. "Twenty-eight years? Did you move to Vienna for college?"

"Yep, and you? I thought you landed with the police?"

"Landed! More like belly-flopped."

A lift of the eyebrows. "How long were you on the force?"

"Nineteen years."

"Nineteen years? What, did you start in kindergarten?"

I don't mean to say that he fell in love with Klara all over again right there on the spot. But he sure remembered what it was about her that he'd fallen for way back when. Because his whole life long, he'd never found another woman who the banter just glided as easy with as Klara from Puntigam High.

Even though she was from the very best of families, as people used to say, doesn't quite add up, Brenner and his family, completely different values.

But on the other hand, they were both from Puntigam, where the beer comes from. And Klara, from the heart of the Puntigam beer family. And beer families, well, maybe their values aren't all that far removed from the simple folk after all.

Even though Klara's family really did take every possible precaution to rid themselves of the smell of hops. Fine upbringing and all. Except Klara didn't hold out for very long at the Swiss boarding school. Of course, she also sang in a Bach choir that rehearsed twice a week back home. And needless to say, she wrinkled that fine little beer-nose of hers at Brenner's taste in music back then.

But otherwise, I've really got to hand it to her. You're not apt to find a person who thought less of herself than Klara. For that kind of money, definitely not. And even when it came to music, I'd like to think it was more Brenner and his over-sensitivity to the timelessness of Jimi Hendrix than it was Klara and her upbringing.

"And what have you been doing these past twenty-eight years in Vienna?"

"I'm a high school music teacher."

"It's not like you need to work, though."

Klara smiled weakly. You know that smile that mon-eyed people get when they're given to understand by some poor chump: With money like yours, you can't possibly have any problems.

It was equally awkward for Brenner that, after three de-cades, it took all of three minutes for a reference to money to slip out of him. And me personally, I'm always the first to say: If a person's got too much money in his pockets, then he can bet the day will come when he'll be swinging from the lamppost. But you've just got to take care of it quietly and professionally, you don't need to be making jealous allusions all the time.

"Birthright's a bitch, huh?" Brenner said, trying to iron out his blunder with something like empathy.

"Deathright's a bitch, too," Klara smiled.

"Deathright?"

Klara looked at him like she always used to when he was slow to catch on. Because needless to say, intelligence-wise, Klara was a tad ahead of him.

Deathright. Brenner gave it some thought. And then it hit him: Deathright. My dear swan. If you're headed to radiation on a day like this and pulling off a joke like that: Hats off.

Con: Brenner couldn't very well skirt the issue now.

"What is it that's wrong, then?" he asked as neutrally as possible.

"Let's just say, a louse ran across my liver."

"Of all things."

"Yep, of all things."

"You'd like to think that only beer can attack your liver—and even then, only if you drink it."

"Why drink it when you can inherit it?"

"You always did worry too much. That your parents were to blame if some poor devil drank himself to death."

"You see, I do need the work. That's why I'm a teacher."

"And what are your chances?"

"With men?"

"With radiation."

"Better than with men."

"Then I've got nothing to worry about," Brenner said, getting choked up. Unbelievable, but he had to make a concerted effort to keep that much-touted lump-in-the-throat from making its way into his vocal cords now. Because he was having a full-blown sentimental attack.

He remembered how he and Klara had parted back then. That pretty friend of Klara's was to blame. Bernadette. She was even a one-time winner of the Miss Bazongas Contest at a ritzy Puntigam disco. But the contest's judge was a well-enough-known former *Schlager* singer from Vienna, who stole Miss Bazongas from Brenner that very same night.

And now, Klara and Brenner were to part again, i.e. they'd arrived at the hospital. Brenner accompanied her up to radiation, and in parting, he asked: "Do you use Rapid Response to get to your treatments very often?"

"Just twice a week."

"Then I'm sure we'll be seeing each other."

"I'm sure we will." She lowered her eyebrows. But Brenner wasn't exactly sure anymore: good sign or bad sign?

"Well, then."

"Well, then."

He would've liked to say something nicer. Nothing occurred to him, though. And that's where the advantage to the marathon substance comes in. Brenner didn't have any more time for melancholy feelings. Because on to the next emergency, straightaway. And somebody else's life story to have to listen to. Over and over, the same old story.

It was only as he was returning to his apartment that evening that the substance subsided a little. He thought of Klara again, and in fact, he couldn't get her off his mind and almost called her. I think it was a maneuver aimed more at distraction, though, because he simply didn't know where to start looking for Lil' Berti. Instead, he stood at the window and looked down at the courtyard. And as he did, he softly whistled this melody.

A strange habit of Brenner's, how he'd often go days whistling some song without even noticing that he was doing so. But then, when he actually did think about what he was whistling, the lyrics to the song were often a perfect match for his situation, even though the lyrics hadn't come to mind at all while he was whistling. I'm talking "Foxy Lady" when he was in love with a redhead, or "I'd Rather Buy Me a Tyrolean Hat" when the barber was cutting his hair, or when, if you really want to know, he had a little performance anxiety.

And believe it or not: a girlfriend once ran out on him because of it. Well, not on account of any performance glitches, but because she couldn't stand his inveterate whistling. So he'd only whistle very softly by sucking in the air. Because, after all, she was no redhead.

And what was it that Brenner was completely unaware he was whistling tonight? Well, it was very telling once again. Because it was a song that Klara had once put on a mix tape for him.

Brenner's apartment was seventy square meters split between two and a half rooms. So if it's a twenty-eight-year-old cassette you're looking for, you'll be searching a long time. Brenner was certain that he still had it somewhere, though. But you know what they say: moving house three times is as good as your house burning down. And over the last few years, Brenner had moved more than just three times. Needless to say, he didn't have half the things that had been lying around his civil service apartment two years ago.

Then again, most things turn back up at some point. But no, that one thing you're looking for, not there. I think it's some kind of law.

And here's another law: nowadays when you move, anything you haven't reached for in years you throw away so that you have less to transport and put away. But Day One in your new apartment, guaranteed, whatever it is, you'll need it desperately and will end up having to buy yourself a new one.

And another law: If there was a detour somewhere, then, guaranteed, Brenner took it. That always made his superiors on the force livid. And sometimes I suspect he did it on purpose. But then I always have to remind myself, he simply cannot concentrate on the essentials. So Brenner, instead of finally searching for Lil' Berti, who was possibly in mortal danger, was now spending hours searching for an old mix tape.

He had a box full of cassettes that were more than twenty years old for the most part. Some even from his school days. And he hadn't opened this box in years.

Because ever since the advent of CDs and all that, nobody listens to cassettes anymore. At most in the car, and a car, well, nobody's even got his own car anymore. And in the ambulance, well, arguing with his co-workers over whose music, no, thank you. The radio is just the right antidote, all day long, for everyone.

He found the box in just a few minutes, and I've got to admit, this is actually a bad example to prove my law now, because, as a matter of fact, everything worked out: He moved it, and he needed it. Wait'll you get a load of this, though.

In the box were fifty if not a hundred cassettes. Nearly two hours in that mess he spent searching around. Then, you put another cassette in and listen to what's on that one, because ancient labeling, and then you flip it over to the B side, and then you spend half an hour winding it—there goes the night.

And this whole time he didn't spend one second thinking about Berti. Some things I just have to shake my head about. You're supposed to be looking for a person, and what do you look for instead, a cassette. And don't you go thinking that if he'd just found the cassette, it would've revealed Berti's whereabouts to him, either.

Because after he'd finally gone through all the tapes in the box, he had to have realized: they were all there, except the one that Klara had made him back in high school. And you see, that's where the law comes back in again.

CHAPTER 10

"I've been cured of men once and for all," Nicole the blood-bank secretary declared, slinging her arm around Brenner.

"I can understand that."

"Why would *you* be able to understand *that*?"

"Because you speak so clearly."

"You really think I speak clearly?" she whispered into his ear. I can't be completely sure if sound waves were even involved, or if it was just a direct transmission from her lips to his eardrum.

Now, I don't want to act like this was somehow unpleasant for Brenner. Or like he was one of those types, i.e. the English gentleman, who as a matter of principle doesn't take advantage of a woman who's had five or six frilly umbrella drinks. Certainly not.

Although Brenner was generally open-minded about taking detours, Nicole was just too much for him right now.

Brenner had spent hours that night at home, looking for the cassette instead of for Berti, when, at a quarter past ten, he decided to head to Floridsdorf and prowl around the Watzek Cement Works a little.

When four men came out, it wasn't exactly hard for Brenner to spot the Pro Med chief. Because he was only half as wide as the three cement workers, and needless to say, the resemblance to his dead brother, uncanny.

Then Stenzl and the fattest of the three cement workers drove off in a white Mercedes, and the other two in a small pickup truck with one of those blue construction tarps. It goes without saying, Brenner would've preferred to ride in the Mercedes, but it was simply less conspicuous in the back of the flatbed under the tarp. The young morgue worker had been annoyed earlier that afternoon when the trailer had obstructed his view, but needless to say, Brenner was grateful for it now.

When the Mercedes and the truck pulled up in front of the Golden Heart and parked, Brenner waited beneath the tarp for five minutes before he, too, went into the Golden Heart. The two workers he spotted right away, but the two from the Mercedes, gone.

Nicole was there, though, and beckoning him to her table. That was at a quarter after eleven, and now it was already twelve-thirty and still bustling at the Golden Heart. And Brenner, still at Nicole's table.

"And why is it that you're through with men, exactly?" he asked her.

"I can understand you asking that," Nicole whispered in his ear. "Because you speak so clearly!"

Even without Nicole there, he probably wouldn't have been able to get a word in with Angelika Lanz—there was still so much commotion at the Golden Heart, what with the Pro Meddlers pokering away their measly lumps of pay. Over the course of just this one night, Brenner would watch as one of them lost 20,000 schillings only to win it all back in a single game. He could actually see the sweat soaking through the man's shirt during that last round.

Unlike for the gambler, though, for Brenner it was quite enjoyable. Because for the first time all evening, the Golden Heart's patrons stared at somebody else. The sweaty poker player from their own ranks instead of the Rapid Responder who had the nerve to set foot back in the Golden Heart before his eye had even healed.

When you look at it that way, Brenner could be grateful that Nicole, who was ordering one florid umbrella drink after another, had latched onto him tonight. And each time one of those drinks got set down in front of her, Brenner would softly whistle this melody to himself. You know, his old malady.

"What're you whistling every time I get a drink?" Nicole asked, annoyed all the sudden. Because when you're drunk, the emotions often run a little high.

"Was I whistling?"

The music at the bar was loud enough that he himself hadn't heard himself whistling, even though he was doing the kind of whistling where you suck the air in. So he was surprised that Nicole had heard him just now.

"Or were you just puckering up like that because you're trying to spit suggestively in my glass?" Nicole said, laughing, practically: best joke I've ever cracked.

But Brenner was curious to know what he was whistling now, and he didn't have to wait for long, because the melody was right back on his lips again. The melody from the cassette that he'd spent hours looking for, for nothing.

"A churchy song."

"A cherry song? What're you whistling a cherry song for when I'm drinking a strawberry daiquiri? You oughta be whistling a strawberry song!" Nicole said, laughing. No physical therapist in the world would've recommended the unnatural maneuver that she contorted herself in just then. She laid her cheek on Brenner's collarbone so that her face was looking down, but those Martian eyes of hers were rolled all the way up so she could look into Brenner's eyes. And only her head seemed to follow suit a little; the rest of her drunken body remained fixed in place, and Brenner was waiting for the sound of her neck snapping at any moment now. But instead what he heard was the sound of her voice pleading with him: "Please! Whistle a strawberry song for me."

"I didn't say cherry song."

"You didn't? Well, you sure didn't say strawberry song, either."

"I said: churchy song. Church. You know, where you drink wine. And not shakes with umbrellas in them."

Okay, I do have to correct Brenner on that. I've been told that there are parishes today that, in an effort to keep up with the trends, are putting umbrellas in their chalices, too.

"So you're into whistling church hymns, huh? Kinky!"

"I wasn't aware that I was."

"So, what kind of church hymns are you into?"

"Forget it."

"Pleeease! Whistle your church song again for me. To see if I can recognize it."

" 'Come, Sweet Death.' "

"Pardon me?"

" 'Come, Sweet Death' is the name of the hymn."

Surely you still remember the first time you got a compass to sketch with in geometry class at school. There's nothing funnier in the middle of class than ramming the compass into the ass of the student sitting in front of you. Well, that's exactly how Nicole jumped now. The last time Brenner had seen anything like it was at Puntigam High after he'd given Walter Neuhold a good compass-tweaking. Practically did the tarantella.

Needless to say, Nicole bolted. One second she's draped along Brenner's collarbone, the next she's sitting about as upright as a candlestick. "Let me get this straight: you watched me order one strawberry daiquiri after another, and each time I did, you whistled 'Come, Sweet Death'? Did you think I would like that?"

"I didn't even notice I was doing it."

"You know, you were sucking down one beer after another, too. So now I'm wondering—between the two of us, who will be the first to meet that sweet death you've been whistling about?"

"Definitely me."

"How can you be so sure about that?"

"C'mon, how could you tell, anyway?"

"Very funny. You think you're pretty clever, don't you?"

Brenner noticed that, little by little, Nicole was getting explosive. Which is why he tried to say something calming now, by telling Nicole that, in all honesty, he simply couldn't get the song out of his head since he'd met Klara.

The In All Honesty method, though, often not the best recipe if you're trying to head off an explosion.

And by the time he noticed that the moment he'd said "Klara," Nicole's eyes actually changed color, it was already too late. "I think you're the one who killed Stenzl," was all she said. "And now I'm going to call the police."

And—cut. Brenner was relieved to have Nicole out the door at last. The snide grins of the Pro Meddlers didn't faze him much, either. Better that than the stony faces of the two cement workers. He briefly debated asking them where their bosses had disappeared off to. But then he got lost in thought again.

It wasn't actually a church song that Klara had taped for him way back then. No, a Passion is what it was called, or so Brenner recalled now. And he imagined what Nicole probably would've said if, instead of saying "church song," he'd said "Passion." The nonsense she would've come up with.

Back in high school, when Klara had taped the song for him, he'd even liked it. Even though his taste at the time: Hendrix Only. And you're going to laugh, but Bach and Jimi Hendrix, not all that different. Jimi Hendrix, a lot of repetition in his music, and Bach, too, always repeating himself. It just keeps going and going, and if you happen to be seventeen, you just float, like you're on a cloud.

Needless to say, though, that was just Brenner, his way of looking at things. Klara had always been more of the Bach expert, what with his fugues and all.

"Come, Sweet Death," though, even in Klara's case, had more to do with puberty than expertise, i.e. everything always being about death or what have you. Because when you're seventeen nowadays, death's got a certain sweetness to it. You're still immortal at seventeen, but because life at seventeen is often bitter, too, you tend to think: death, sweet by comparison. And when you're from a certain Puntigam milieu, death doesn't just mean death but dying a great death. But when you're fifty and going to radiation therapy, death: just sucks.

I can't tell now, is Brenner just lost deep in thought, or is he actually falling asleep a little. And it wouldn't be any wonder if he was. After three weeks straight of work, those two beers were making him sleepy. Anyway, all of the sudden the poker-playing Pro Meddlers and the cement workers were gone, and he found himself alone with Angelika Lanz.

"Back again, eh?" Angelika said.

"I've been trying to get ahold of you for a few days."

"I haven't been home much lately."

"I gathered."

"My father's sentencing was the day before yesterday."

Angelika had on a silver Lycra top and shiny black Lycra pants. And emblazoned across her belt buckle in gold letters: "ESCAPADE," a little excessive, if you ask me.

"That's what I heard," Brenner said.

"That's the best you can do?" Angelika still thought she was the one who could be bold here.

"I don't think you'd like to hear the other thing."

Angelika lit a cigarette: "And what would that be?"

"That would be: Why didn't you tell me anything about your father's gambling debts?"

"So?"

"So where were you really on the afternoon that Bimbo got strangled with his own gold chain?"

Angelika exhaled her cigarette so violently, you could've swatted a fly with the smoke. So Brenner wasn't surprised when the recoil flung her head back on her neck. "Don't make me laugh," she said, exhaling the rest.

"Wouldn't be the first time that a father stuck out his neck for his daughter."

"You're right about that. My father really didn't do it."

"I don't think your father did it, either. He's much too weak to have strangled Bimbo."

"But you think that I'm capable of doing it?" she said with a laugh.

"Not capable of doing it, but of knowing something about it."

Angelika emptied the ashtrays into a trash can and the trash can into a massive trash bag. Then she placed the trash bag into a dumbwaiter. There's no food at the Golden Heart, but it used to be a restaurant upstairs here where the Golden Heart is today, and down in the basement was the kitchen. Then, renovated ten times, and these days the dumbwaiter's a trash waiter.

"Up until two days ago my father's account had negative eight hundred thousand schillings in it. And seven hundred thousand of them he still owed to Bimbo."

Meanwhile Angelika turned on the dishwasher and sealed the open wine bottles with those ghastly rubber stoppers. It struck Brenner that she'd had to develop very deft finger movements so as not to break her five-centimeter-long nails.

"As of two days ago, his account's settled. And Bimbo's ex-wife withdrew her complaint."

Brenner was just having a musical day today, I guess, because he nearly broke out into song now—"Who's gonna pay for the next round? Who called the waitress, yo-ho! Which of you's got enough cabbage? Which of you's got enough dough?"—but, thankfully, he just recited the lyrics.

"I wondered about that, too," Angelika said, dismally. But I don't know: dismal because of the matter at hand or dismal because of the dopey song he'd just recited.

"That means," Brenner said like a normal person again, "your father will get eight years—four on the grounds that Bimbo tyrannized and provoked him. And after two he'll be out on good behavior and free of debt."

Angelika rinsed out the ice-cube trays, filled them with fresh water, and put them back in the freezer.

"Million and a half in two years. Your father never earned that much."

"Me neither."

"And you don't happen to know who paid off his debt for him?"

"How should I know that?"

"You live with us, and you work for Pro Med. You must've heard something."

"Whoever paid's probably the person who's got Bimbo's murder on his conscience."

There are some people who you just don't know about: do they just act dumb or are they just really that naïve? What are you supposed to do, step on their toes a little or meekly carry on the conversation?

"Have you ever heard anything about Rupprechter?" Brenner said, venturing a change of topic.

"For as long as I can remember, my father cursed her name."

"That sounds about right." Brenner took a cigarette from Angelika's pack, even though he hadn't smoked a single one since he'd started working as an EMT. "Irmi was Rupprechter's in-home nurse."

"Yeah, I know," Angelika said and gave him a light.

"You know everything."

"I live with you guys, I work here. A person hears a thing or two."

"Why didn't you tell me?"

"Tell you that Irmi was Rupprechter's in-home nurse? What's so important about that?"

Brenner took just two drags and put his cigarette out.

"She worked for twenty other old bags, too," Angelika said with a shrug.

She put a couple of empty beer bottles in a case, then put that case on top of another case of beer, and then shoved both cases with her foot across the stone floor. As she did, they emitted that shrieking chalkboard sound.

"Rupprechter told me that Irmi was snooping around her house."

It automatically sounded a little intense, the way he said it, even though if he was talking any louder, it was only to drown out the shrieking.

"Well, if that's all she did," Angelika said, walking back. "She also could've lifted a million off her passbook every time she was there without Rupprechter ever knowing it. Wouldn't have been the first time that a nurse helped herself to some helpless old bag's purse."

"Nevertheless. I asked around a little. And Irmi was snooping around on a couple of her other patients, too."

"As far as I'm concerned, why shouldn't she? What do you want with her, anyway? She was just an innocent by-stander." Angelika was beginning to run out of patience. "That girl was cursed with bad luck all her life."

"How is it you know so much about her?"

Angelika emptied the olives out of a glass bowl and into a plastic one and put the lid on it. You know, those plastic containers that people used to sell at their own parties and the housewives would come over and buy them all up, and then they couldn't manage the household's money, and so divorce and so on, but the containers—sure are practical.

"I work here."

"And you live with us."

She put the container in the refrigerator, and I've just got to add: If the leftovers lasted longer than the marrige, well, also not exactly the inventors—marriage, I meant to say. Not exactly the inventors of Tupperware—you see, that's what it's called.

"Irmi used to go out with one of my father's co-workers."

"With who?"

"You didn't know him."

She wiped down the bar with a pink Clorox wipe, then tossed it into the newly emptied trashcan. Then she gave her fingers a sniff and made a face and said, "I don't know anymore what his name was. Everybody called him Lun-gauer. Even though he wasn't even from Lungau, but from Burgenland. No clue how he got that name."

"And he left Irmi sitting on the shelf?"

"No, they even wanted to get married. Made a good pair, in fact. I have to say, he was one of the nicer ones."

"And?"

She washed her hands, wiped them on her pants, and then gave her fingers another sniff. "That Clorox smell, crazy, you just can't get it off your fingers. Lungauer always drove the seven-forty. Not the new one, though. Before they got the new one, the seven-forty was the oldest one. Practically every week it needed some kind of repair. But Lungauer was a skilled mechanic and did most of the repairs himself. In return, he always got stuck driving that old wreck because it saved Junior so much in repair costs."

"How long since he stopped working?"

"For a good year maybe."

"Did he get into an accident?"

"Didn't get into one but one got into him."

"Didn't get into one but one got into him? What, did a dictionary explode somewhere? Why is it I'm dealing with nothing but quibblers today?"

One thing you can't forget. The whole strawberry-song incident was still weighing heavily on him.

"This one time, he was repairing a tailpipe with another guy. It wasn't even on his vehicle. But he was the kind of guy to help out." Angelika counted the packs of cigarettes and took the cash out of the cigarette drawer. "Anyway, there was this screw that was completely melted on. That's why the other driver needed someone to help him. So the two of them are standing under the hydraulic lift. Lungauer's holding the tailpipe in place, and the other guy's chiseling away with the screwdriver with all he's got. Then, he loses his grip, and the screwdriver goes straight into Lungauer's right eye."

"Holy shit!"

"And all the way in, right into his brain."

"Shit." The mere idea of it hurt so much that he nearly yelped.

"You can say that again."

"Shit," Brenner said very quietly.

Needless to say, not a pleasant thought. And even if you've often carelessly said that somebody's got a screw loose, most of the time you'd never wish on them that it get tightened back up with a screwdriver.

"Did he survive?"

"Survived, sure. But severely disabled. Wheelchair. And mentally, too. Just vegetating. You know how people say they should've let somebody die. He can't even talk right anymore, doesn't understand anything at all."

Brenner was so engrossed in the story that he didn't say anything for a little while.

But then, he did want to know something. "Who was the other guy?"

Lanz's daughter arranged the liquor bottles in a row in front of her: strawberry, raspberry, kiwi, cacao.

"Bimbo."

Shit, Brenner thought.

Angelika measured the schnapps levels in the bottles with a wooden ruler and then recorded the results in a notebook with graph-paper pages.

All the way in, right into his brain.

The very thought of it was so painful that Brenner nearly

yelped again. The very thought was drilling itself all the way in, right into his brain.

The very thought that, from the outset, the bullet had been meant for Irmi. That the murderer only shot through Stenzl as a cover up for his real target.

"What're you whistling?" Angelika asked, while she wrote in the notebook.

"No idea," Brenner said.

Even though it'd been some time since he'd had such a horrible idea as he did at that very moment.

CHAPTER 11

As Brenner shook Angelika's hand goodbye at the Golden Heart, he made an interesting discovery: nowadays when you're a detective and you think about death too much, it can easily come to pass that death thinks about you, too, for a change.

Although I've been told that death has a cold hand. And the hand throttling Brenner's neck now was a warm hand. And the hand twisting his arm behind his back felt perfectly normal, too. Human, I mean, though not humane, because when somebody half-dislocates your shoulder, you can't well call him humane, regardless of his temperature. And as for that somebody's kneecap, it wasn't its coldness that especially stood out to Brenner, either, but its hardness, beneath which his rib instantly snapped like the flimsiest of toothpicks.

Interesting, though! It wasn't his ribs where he first felt it. Only when he breathed. Better put: attempted to breathe, i.e. choking fit.

Which is why Brenner briefly confused the two cement workers for death now. Even though it's not like the Watzek drivers beat him to death. They just stuffed him in the cramped dumbwaiter. Descent into hell, Brenner thought, when it let him off down in the basement below the Golden Heart.

It was much nicer down below than it was up above, like a poker salon in Las Vegas, you've got to picture it. Plush and mirrors and everything. Me personally, I've never been to Las Vegas. Television, though. I went to a Vegas bar in Salzburg once, and believe it or not, at four in the morning, I met a blind woman there.

Maybe that'd make a more interesting story, but unfortunately not suitable for all audiences. Anyway, where was I? The Vegas salon beneath the Golden Heart. It was roughly as large as the Rapid Responder's Kellerstüberl, but considerably more elegant. With a humongous pool table like they have in England. Drive on the left, oversized pool tables, and princes with ears that jut out, there's a people for you. But please. The pool table in the basement of the Golden Heart, nobody was playing on it anyway tonight.

The men were sitting around a card table and were passing a cup of dice around: the Watzek boss, in the flesh. The Pro Med chief, in the flesh. And Berti, in the flesh.

"Glad you could finally make it," the Pro Meddler said and gave the cup a shake. "We're a man short."

Because Berti wasn't playing. It's hard to do when your hands are shackled to a pool table. Interesting, though! When you put Lil' Berti, with his six-plus feet, next to the English billiards table, the proportions looked all right.

As Brenner squeezed himself out of the dumbwaiter, he was afraid his broken rib might be protruding from his chest, and the Watzek boss might mistake his rib for the barrel of a gun and shoot him, i.e. self-defense. But thank

god, his rib wasn't sticking out. It was just a subjective illu-
sion, triggered by the pain.

And then old Watzek personally verified whether
Brenner was armed. Even though, needless to say, the workers already took his Glock off him upstairs in the Golden
Heart. But "Security Is Security," that was Watzek's slogan,
and Watzek stood by it in private, too. You've got to picture
it roughly like open-heart surgery, but without the anesthe-
sia. And with a roughneck instead of a surgeon, mucking
around in your rack of broken ribs instead of your ticker.

Stenzl, though, was all the more polite for it. He pulled
up a chair for Brenner and started right in on the dice, as
though Brenner were an old craps buddy.

"Forty-three," he said and nudged the cup to Brenner.

In the police academy, thank god, they used to shoot
dice all night long. Brenner knew exactly what he had to
do now. Because even if maybe he'd forgot just about everything else from the academy, the rules of shooting dice you
don't forget.

Just like how you don't unlearn how to swim, or the Our
Father, let's say, or skiing. Shake the cup, pop it down on
the table, and take a peek under it so only you can see what
number you rolled. Then you say the number, and the others
have to guess whether you're lying or not—you don't forget
a thing like that.

And I think it's somewhat justified, them giving the
dice such high priority at the police academy. Because when
you're passing the cup, the next guy's got to roll an even
higher number than the previous guy did with his two
dice. When your predecessor rolls a four and a two, he says

"forty-two," and then you've got to roll at least forty-three. And if you roll at least forty-three, then everything's okay, and you pass the cup to the next guy, and he's got to roll something higher, and so on, around the circle.

Now, the art of it is when you roll something lower than your predecessor, i.e. poker face. You've sneaked a look under the cup, and now you've simply got to declare a higher number.

Now, your fellow players have a choice: they can either believe you or not. If one of them doesn't, and he lifts your cup and catches you in your lie, then you pay. I know people who've lost house and home that way. But if your fellow player lifts up your cup and you weren't lying, then he's the one who loses it all, that's the joke.

And that's why I say, they were right to place such importance on rolling dice at the police academy. Because needless to say, great parallels to life, how you've always got to amass more and more, bluffing and all that, and ultimately, somebody lifts up your cup and it's *Auf wiedersehen*.

You can study police psychology for ten years and learn only half as much about life as you can in ten nights spent rolling the dice.

Brenner shook the cup, placed it on the table, looked underneath, and said: "twenty-two."

Because needless to say: double digits beat out any mixed digits, and they even have their own name: doubles.

"I've always wanted to roll with Junior's crew of thugs," the Pro Med chief said, as Watzek took the cup from Brenner.

"I can't hear anything out of this ear since your stooges

beat me up," Brenner replied. Although it almost made him sick, how the tremor caused by speaking spurred his rib into his lung.

"Then you'll have to tell him," the Pro Med chief signaled to Watzek. But without even batting an eye. He was still shaking the dice, like some kind of Brazilian rhythm machine. And truly, in his fat paws, the cup looked more like a toy tumbler in the hand of a giant baby.

"If I'd known at the time that it wouldn't keep you from snooping around like some dummkopf, you wouldn't be able to hear out of the other ear, either," the Pro Meddler said. "And you wouldn't be able to see. Or smell, either. Or taste anymore."

"But, feel? I'd still be able to feel?" Brenner inquired.

"I'm afraid you're going to be laughing on the other side of your face before the day is out."

"What do you want to play for, Herr Stenzl?" Brenner thought it better to stick to formalities. Because these days, people rush headlong into first names, and then it's not so convenient anymore when one of those first names ends up being your boss, say, or your murderer, because those are two categories of people that have a natural propensity for disrespect.

"Who we'll shoot first," the Pro Meddler said, with a thin-lipped smile. "You or your companion."

Now, on the inside, Brenner was heaving a sigh of relief. Of course, sighing's the worst thing you can do for a broken rib. But better a little rib *Schmerz* than death *Schmerz*. And if you're going to be spoiled for choice, that one's a no-brainer.

Don't go thinking he sighed out of some hope that they'd

at least shoot Lil' Berti first. He sighed because, old saying: As long as a dog's barking, it's not shooting.

"Double fours," Watzek announced, and then slid the cup past Berti and over to the Pro Meddler. I mean, no manners—just because Berti's hands weren't on the table.

Double fours, needless to say, this is the critical moment. Where, whether you want to or not, you almost always have to lift the cup. Because the likelihood of beating out a forty-four without bluffing, practically nil.

The Pro Meddler didn't lift the cup, though, but went right ahead and shook it. And as he did, he said, "But first there's something I want to know from you."

"About your brother's murder?"

"You all know for a fact that I'm not behind my brother's murder."

"You kicked your brother out, and as a result, Junior saw to it that he got the top job at the blood bank. Now you're afraid that the whole blood business is going to go to Vienna Rapid Response."

"And what exactly do you think the Sport Coats United have been doing these past four weeks? They've turned the whole operation on its head three times. Didn't find a thing, though!" the Pro Meddler said, flicking at the dirt under his fingernail. "And Junior knows that just as well as I do."

"Who do you think killed your brother, then?"

"I have no idea how many dirty dealings he was mixed up in. Somebody finally had enough."

"You were just doing the humane thing by kicking him out."

"That's right. Or else I would've had to shoot him myself.

He's no use to me dead, though. Then again, he'd been hold-ing out on me for some time now with Junior's books."

"What sort of books?"

"Don't act so stupid. You think I don't know what you're looking for from me?"

"There was never any talk of books—just radio. Junior wanted to know if you were tapping ours."

Sheer agony now. Old Watzek and the Pro Meddler got such a kick out of Brenner's plea that Brenner almost had to laugh along with them. And anybody who's ever laughed with a broken rib knows exactly what that means.

But then, from one moment to the next, the Pro Med-dler, dead serious: "I'm going to let you in on something now. For years we've been tapping Rapid Response's ra-dio. And for years you Rapid Responders have tapped ours. We're in complete agreement! It's best for both sides. Like with enemy states, where it's actually the mutual espionage that secures the peace. So that both sides always know ex-actly where they stand. Not peace exactly, but a cease-fire."

It's a very interesting thing, a broken rib like this. A fit of laughter or a fit of rage, doesn't matter which, because the physicality of either will bring on the pain. But that it should sting every bit as much if you repress your temper and don't move at all as it does if you express your temper and fly off the handle—now that's interesting. Because even though Brenner was sitting there as calmly as a yoga teacher, his rib was blowing its top so bad that he was about ready to hit the ceiling from the pain.

He couldn't know whether the Pro Meddler was taking him for a ride or not. Whether this whole radio-tapping mission of Junior's was justified or not. But you see, in that regard, a rib is often more discerning than its owner.

"All right, out with the truth finally," the Pro Meddler said, still not announcing the number he'd rolled. "Or would you call it a coincidence that around the same time as my brother's murder, two Rapid Response snoops turn up here? Although I have to say: Your excuse with the radio tapping is so lame that it almost gives me something to think about."

"What do you want to know?"

"I want to know how much you know."

Brenner didn't say anything. His chest was hurting him so bad now that it would've almost been easier for Berti, with his mouth taped shut, to say something.

But there was something else the Pro Meddler had to say now, anyway. Because there are only three possible rolls that can beat double-fours. Either double-fives. Or double-sixes.

"Max," the Pro Meddler said.

Some believe "Max" is short for Maximilian. But when you're rolling dice, needless to say, it's short for maximum. Because when you roll a twenty-one, there's nothing higher, it is the absolute maximum, established by somebody at some point in time, and it still applies today. First the usual combinations, then the doubles, then twenty-one, and then nothing else.

Now for some intricacies to the rules of the game. Because the game's not over yet. And that's why I say, good police training. Because maxed out and still a chance.

Watch closely, this gets complicated. When a player says "max," there are still several possibilities for the next guy up.

In concrete terms: either Brenner lifts the cup and if it

turns out that the Pro Meddler's lied, then the Pro Meddler loses the game.

Or, Brenner lifts the cup, and the Pro Meddler really does have twenty-one, in which case Brenner loses.

Or, third possibility: Brenner doesn't even look under the cup, but passes it unseen to Watzek. And then Watzek has to look under the cup, whether he wants to or not.

And then, that opens up two more possibilities. Either there really is twenty-one under the cup, in which case Watzek loses, because he called bluff when there was no bluff.

Or, what's much more probable is that the Pro Meddler lied. In that case, though, it's not the Pro Meddler who loses, but the middle man, i.e. Brenner, because he was too cowardly to lift the damn cup up himself, and instead sat there cooling his hemorrhoids between two chairs, so to speak.

So many possibilities. And yet, not one came to pass.

Because the Pro Meddler gets up and calls for the dumbwaiter now: "Until I know how much my brother told Junior, you two are staying put down here," he said. "The dumbwaiter's the only exit. And we'll be putting it out of service. Until something occurs to you."

Brenner debated whether or not he should explain to Stenzl that his brother hadn't been the target of the murder at all, that in truth it'd been all about Irmi. But, A of all, impossible that he would've believed him anyway. And B of all, the Pro Meddler had other concerns. And I don't mean Junior's books. No, all of the sudden, he had completely different concerns.

As he talked to Brenner, he was standing with his back

to the dumbwaiter. That's why he didn't see at first what Brenner was already seeing. That the dumbwaiter wasn't empty. But crammed full like a can of sardines. With two fat cement workers.

The one had his arms bound behind his back with his own belt, which at least didn't look quite as ridiculous. But the other one's arms were bound into a cross by a belt on which sparkled the golden letters: ESCAPADE.

Because needless to say, it's just not possible for some fat cement worker to have a knee so sharp that it instantly breaks your rib. The cement worker's knee only felt as sharp as it did upstairs in the Golden Heart because between his knee and Brenner's rib was Brenner's Glock in the breast pocket of his coat. And when you've got the knee of a hundred-kilo cement worker pressing against your pistol, a rib like that's nothing.

Needless to say, the cement workers stripped him of his Glock right away. That part they did very well. It's just that they shouldn't have left it lying around the Golden Heart. The cement workers were commonplace goons who'd never touched a gun in their lives. In their heart of hearts, well, these were two decent-hearted people.

Needless to say, it was Angelika who'd overpowered them with the gun in her hand. First, she forced the one to tie up the other at gunpoint, and then she tied up the second one herself with her ESCAPADE belt. Because the buckle had this very special mechanism, and just like that, you're lickety-click defenseless.

While the two cement workers were sheepishly explaining the whole story to the Pro Meddler and Watzek, the dumbwaiter started back up again.

And interesting! Compared to the meaty cement work-er's knee, Brenner's Glock was something pointy, sharp, and rib-cracking, but in Angelika's delicate hand it had the effect of something crude and ungainly.

Angelika handed Brenner back his Glock. And no sooner were her hands free then, *vzzzzt*, she'd sliced through the duct tape on Berti's wrists with her own fingernails.

The Pro Meddler looked about as embittered as if some-body had completely amputated his lips. And I have to say, given the circumstances, understandable.

Because the plan was supposed to be for him and Watzek to be on their way and for the cement workers to take the dumbwaiter out of service and for Brenner and Berti to be left there in the basement stewing over Stenzl's question.

And now it was Angelika who had moved her dumb-waiter to checkmate.

And now it was the Pro Meddler and the Watzek men who would sit stewing in the basement of the Golden Heart until the following night.

CHAPTER 12

In recent years, there's been a lot of ballyhoo about the moon—crimes of passion and how the moon affects your haircut, your love life, and what have you. And how there are more car accidents when there's a full moon, well, we've always known that.

Interesting, though, how these things we've always known always turn out to be wrong. Because statistics and that sort of thing have proven: actually fewer car accidents when there's a full moon because the light's better. And when you drive an ambulance you don't even need statistics because your own experience has shown: moon, zero effect. Based on the number of calls, there are other things you've felt way more. Let me break it down for you: humidity, *ja*, high pressure weather system, *ja*, the Föhn winds, *ja*, moon, *nein*.

And the real triggers are in another class altogether, i.e. start of summer vacation, i.e. college rejection letters and teenage suicide, i.e. Danube Isle Fest with all its alcohol-poisoned cadavers. They've got nothing to do with a full moon.

But the fact that this year the Danube Isle Fest would fall on a full moon of all things, needless to say, double-threat.

Because that way the politicians could blame everything on the full moon again.

And another thing that's got nothing to do with the full moon. The fact that Brenner—after Angelika and Berti had bandaged up his rib, and he sent the two of them off to bed—couldn't fall asleep.

"Hello?" Klara finally picked up after he'd let it ring at least ten times.

"Well, aren't we up late," Brenner said, taking the bull by the horns, as it were.

"Simon." Klara breathed a sigh of relief.

"Nobody's called me that in a long time," Brenner said, because around EMTs, of course, only last names or nicknames, and Nicole had taken to calling him Brenni, terrible, but such things do happen in this life.

"Are you in one of your sentimental moods again?" She gave a big yawn, and still half-yawning, she said: "Allow me to console you. It'll all get better after two a.m. Two was always when your sentimental moods peaked."

"You seem to know your way around them pretty well."

"I've often found myself up at night lately."

Brenner thought his sentimental mood might be making advances on Klara.

But instead, Klara, rather unsentimental: "So, what do you want?"

"Back when we used to fight, you always thought a good deal of your logic."

"Compared to yours, it was hardly an art."

"You always said that music and logic activate the same part of the brain."

Klara had to laugh. "I think neuroscientists have got a little farther in the meantime. They'd almost have to, judging from the logical development of my own life."

"You can't go claiming the opposite when it's your logic that I need right now," Brenner said.

"Why do I get the feeling you just need somebody to talk to?"

"Are talking and logic linked, too, I mean, brain-wise?"

"If you're any example, then, no, not likely," Klara said, laughing. "But you can come by sometime, and we can talk."

"It's just—it'd have to be now."

"You never could wait," Klara said, rubbing his nose in it. And frankly, that was a little unfair, because Brenner was actually a very patient person. Too patient, you might say.

But then, when he had to wait three whole minutes outside for a taxi, he nearly hit the roof. But then, the ride went fast, because never is there so little traffic in this city as at two-thirty in the morning.

And thank god, you've got to admit. Because as the black Mondeo and the red GTI flew past the taxi, there might've been a few deaths if there'd been any traffic.

"Those lunatics!" the taxi driver yelled. "They're going to smash their own skulls on the next median!"

That was another cause of accidents that as an EMT you saw more prevalently of late. The kamikaze duel between the newly licensed rookie drivers. Because it'd become something of a fad the last couple of years for rookie drivers to race each other in their souped-up vehicles on the empty streets at night. I'm just saying, Golf GTI and tinted windows and spoilers and grills and personalized license plates and Red Bull and, and, and—the laminate's still cooling on their driver's licenses.

"Otherwise pretty quiet today, though," Brenner said, hoping to calm the taxi driver down. Because for a moment he was afraid she might pursue the two lunatics.

"The night before Danube Isle Fest is always quiet."

"People saving themselves for the big party." Because Brenner, always a bit of a psychologist.

"But every day there are more and more kamikaze drivers," the taxi driver said, shaking her head.

"Even though practically every day one of them gets laid up."

"It doesn't help." The taxi driver thumped her steering wheel. "For every one that dies, there are three new ones to take his place. Like with moths, you might be able to kill one, but you can never kill the eggs."

In Döbling, where Klara lived, it was so quiet that Brenner almost thought better of opening the garden gate. She sure didn't pay for this house with what she made as a teacher, Brenner thought as she came out to greet him. Because needless to say, envy like that's almost as tough to get rid of as all the kamikaze drivers.

Klara was normally dressed, though, I mean, not some god-awful millionairess's leisure suit as the respectable address might've suggested. But more like she'd just got home from school. Because nowadays teachers can wear jeans, too, and with Klara it was completely justified, because still a terrific figure.

"You're looking much better today," Brenner said, and it really was his honest opinion.

"Two-thirty in the morning's my best time," Klara said, with a coy smile.

What Brenner would've liked most was just to start right in on his case. But needless to say, out of politeness, he asked about her health first. And as tends to happen when somebody doesn't really want to say something, it ends up coming out too fast. "What came of the exam?" he asked before he was even through the door.

But Klara took her time showing him in and then offered him a place to sit in her living room before she said: "At my first exam six months ago, the doctor said my chances were 'fifty-fifty.'"

"And in English, no less."

"Yeah, these days doctors just don't speak Latin anymore. Actually, he said it in German: *Fünfzig Prozent.* I just thought fifty-fifty sounded better."

"Fifty-fifty, like two outlaws taking a fifty-fifty split after robbing a bank."

"Exactly. As if there's something to be won in any case. You know, when you're sick, you're constantly having to console healthy people."

"Look who you're talking to. The sick even have to console the ambulance drivers."

"Would you like something to drink?"

"I'd like to know what the doctor said at this visit, not the one six months ago."

"Whisky, maybe?"

"Unbelievable what lushes doctors are," Brenner said in deliberate misunderstanding so that she'd finally come out with it.

"Ninety percent," Klara was beaming.

"Alcohol?"

"Chance at recovery."

"Then you'll be out robbing banks again in no time," Brenner said quickly. Even without the whisky, he really had to swallow a few times before he could get anything else out. "All that about two in the morning isn't true, you know."

"What about two in the morning?"

"You said on the phone that sentimental moods peak at two, and it all gets better from there."

"And it does—only gradually. Not instantly, the way you men always imagine everything changing."

"I see."

"Out with it. What did you come here for?"

"I've had a relapse into some detective work. A murder. And I'm standing all of a millimeter away from the solution, and I can't see it."

"Maybe you need to take a step back so that you can see it." Klara laughed. "I must sound like an old schoolmarm."

"Easier said than done, taking a step back. You can only take a step back if you know what's behind you."

"Maybe it'd be best if you just tell me, so I can solve it all, just like that," Klara said with a snap of her fingers.

"That's roughly how I imagined it going, too."

Then Brenner told her how Bimbo had been strangled with his own gold chain. And the story of Bimbo and Angelika Lanz in the Kellerstüberl the night before his murder. And how the police had arrested old Lanz.

"Well, it's understandable," Klara said.

"What about it's understandable?"

"Why they'd suspect him."

"And what's not understandable?"

"Why you've made it your concern."

Then Brenner told her how, after the incident with the sandler, Junior tasked him with finding out whether Pro Med was tapping their radio. And he told her how Junior had implied that Brenner might be to blame for Bimbo's murder. And how the Pro Meddlers had possibly murdered Bimbo out of retaliation for Brenner's clumsy snooping.

"Pro Med would have to have some real skeletons in the closet to fight back with that kind of brutality, though," Klara said, delighting in her own cleverness.

And so, Brenner just came out with the whole story, how the brother of the Pro Med chief had got shot just two weeks ago. And how his girlfriend had got shot along with him. And how it was Bimbo of all people who'd been the eyewitness to the deed.

"Now it's getting complicated," Klara said.

"That's just the beginning. Because while I was off investigating Pro Med's radio, the Pro Med chief was suspecting me of actually investigating him on account of his finances. And the police were suspecting him of being behind the deaths of both his brother and Bimbo."

And then Brenner disclosed the story that Angelika had just told him a few hours earlier. How Irmi, who'd been accidentally shot, had been the girlfriend of Lungauer, whose eye accidentally got a spike driven into it by Bimbo of all people.

"Accidentally again," Klara said.

"Accidentally Irmi and accidentally her boyfriend."

"Do you mean, two accidentallys equals one deliberately?"

Brenner shrugged his shoulders. "Between the two of us, you're the logician."

"Well, purely in logical terms, two accidents don't necessarily indicate intent. But purely in intuitive terms ..."

"Can you imagine," Brenner said, interrupting her intuitive silence, "if the bullet was actually meant for the seemingly innocent bystander?"

"And all Stenzl had to do was move his head like so, and voilà, the motive's covered up? But what would that mean, then?"

"Exactly. That's what I'm asking you for. You know I've always had a hard time when it comes to concentrating."

"Would you like some coffee?"

Because old superstition, coffee's good for the concentration. And the opposite's true, too. That I can personally attest to.

But the truth is never that simple, yet another important rule. People often come along and curry favor by claiming that the truth is simple. But, take note, the truth is complicated.

As far as coffee goes, for example, what's true is that drinking coffee is lethal for your concentration. Making coffee, on the other hand, staggeringly good for your concentration. There are so many little handles involved in making a cup of coffee, and that's the best concentration aid that there is in this world. Because if you don't drink coffee, generally speaking, you're not making coffee, either, and you see, there it is: the truth.

Now don't go thinking that the truth occurred to Klara as she made coffee for the two of them, like some kind of reacquaintance gift to Brenner—or to celebrate her ninety-percent chance at recovery, ta-da, your culprit.

But as they were standing there in the kitchen, and Klara was getting the coffee going, all the sudden she asked: "What's that you're whistling?"

"Was I whistling?"

The way she smiled at Brenner gave him goose bumps, which, after a certain stage of manhood, is actually quite unpleasant when you factor in feelings and all. And then she said: "You always did have that habit. I only had to think of the lyrics that went to the tune you were whistling, and I'd know exactly where your shoe was pinching you."

"Did I do that back in Puntigam, too?"

Klara puckered her lips. Brenner was thinking she was about to give him one of those obliging aren't-you-precious kisses on the cheek. But instead she just whistled.

"What are you whistling?" he asked. At first he didn't recognize it because, naturally, she whistled the melody so correctly that it was almost unrecognizable.

And now Klara softly began to sing, her voice a little strained from the treatments: "Come, sweet cross."

"Come, sweet death," Brenner corrected her.

But Klara went and fetched a cassette and played it for him, and needless to say: Come, sweet cross. As it turns out, Brenner listened to way too much Jimi Hendrix in his youth and not nearly enough St. Matthew's Passion.

"You once put that on a tape for me."

"I know," Klara smiled.

"And ever since I saw you the other day, the melody hasn't left my head. When I learned how ill you are—it gave me such a scare. I even tore my apartment upside down looking for that tape."

"You'd be searching a long time," Klara grinned. "This is that cassette." She pointed at the stereo.

Because there are certain things in our lives, which we often work out in such a way that they won't be as painful as the unadulterated truth. It's only human, really. Only problem: as time goes by, we actually start to believe in the adulterated version.

Needless to say, after nearly three decades, it came back to Brenner now. That he hadn't left Klara because of Miss Bazongas. No, Klara had kicked him to the curb. After he'd left behind at her house for the third time the cassette she'd made for him. Which she'd gone to painstaking effort for weeks to put together for him. Because it was a recording of her singing in her choir.

Because to Brenner, Klara's delusions about Bach had always just been a matter of pretense, i.e. let's go listen to the St. Matthew's Passion in my room.

"It's not the complete St. Matthew's Passion anyway," Klara explained. "At the time we only sang selections from it, of course. On 'O Sacred Head Sore Wounded,' we even sang all the verses of the medieval poem that aren't even part of the St. Matthew's Passion."

This interested Brenner less now. On the other hand, generous of Klara to divert so elegantly from their awkward history.

When the coffee was ready, Brenner said: "Your Bach's not going to help me find the murderer, either. And I've only got about fourteen hours. Because, by that point, they will have found the Pro Meddlers in the basement of the Golden Heart, and when they do, I'll be counting my lucky stars they don't beat me to death with their dice-rolling fists."

"You know what being sick has made me realize?"

"And here I thought you'd be the last sick person to have any realizations," Brenner said, acting a little crass. "You wouldn't believe it. When you drive an ambulance, practically all you meet's philosophers who've realized something. How is it that as long as a person's healthy, he never gets around to thinking?"

"And here I thought you were the person who wanted to find a murderer," Klara said, getting him back.

She poured two cups of coffee, and they took them back into the living room.

"When the doctor told me about my fifty percent, I gave that number a great deal of thought. Fifty percent. Half. Really quite simple. I remembered a game that I'd made up back when I was still in high school."

"You came up with this when you were in high school? How'd that go? In life we're often deceiving ourselves fifty percent of the time or something?"

"That sounds about right for high school. It's really only during puberty that you'd come up with stuff like that."

"Or when you revisit puberty at three in the morning."

"Back then, I often found it to be the case that the people

I didn't like at first were the very ones who ended up becoming my best friends later. And other people who struck me straightaway as—"

"I'd rather not know right now which category I fell under."

"I became convinced at the time," she said, ignoring him, "that, at the end of the day, fifty percent of the decisions we make turn out to be just plain wrong. But if only it were fifty-one percent, then basically it'd be wiser for you to always do the opposite of what initially seems right to you."

"And why haven't you adhered to this?"

"Why indeed? It was the first illuminating decision that I didn't allow myself to adhere to even though I wanted to."

"Life gets complicated."

"Well, life won't let itself be tricked. You've just got to muddle through all the crap it slings at you."

You see, a few sips of coffee and already their concentration's shot to hell. Nevertheless, Brenner and Klara took a stab at the fifty-percent theory, applying it to the murder case and adopting the overall-least-right opposite solution. But they didn't get much beyond the possibility of Stenzl, in an unparalleled acrobatic feat, nailing himself with a bullet to his own neck.

As Brenner was finally making his way to the door, Klara said: "It's already dawn."

"Don't remind me," Brenner grumbled.

In parting she gave him one of those obliging aren't-you-precious kisses on the cheek after all. Which pressed on his rib a little in the process, but at least it helped Brenner not to get too sentimental.

Their parting words, however, could've just as easily been kept to themselves, as far as Brenner was concerned: "What ever happened to that nice Jason King mustache of yours?"

And be honest: after all these years, would you like to be reminded of a blond Jason King mustache? Because to tell you the truth, he would've impressed even his colleagues at the Rapid Response with that one. But I say, let's forget about it. After thirty years, even a blond Jason King mustache has got to exceed some statute of limitations.

Brenner decided to walk home, even though it took him nearly an hour. He felt like he wasn't going to get any sleep now anyway. And so a walk home at the break of day, well, there's something to be said for that, too.

"Don't remind me," he said, half to himself, half to the pale full moon.

But before anything could dawn on Brenner, two people would have to die first.

It's often said that the city of Vienna is a particularly good place to die. And I don't doubt that. Me personally, though, I happen to think Vienna is a particularly good place to go for a walk. Especially in these parts of the city, where it's a bit hilly. That way, you can take turns, straining this muscle first, then that one, so you don't get tired as fast as you do when it's flat.

And needless to say, it was pleasant for Brenner to be walking along Döblinger's hilly streets at four-thirty in the morning. It almost seemed to him as if the magnificent houses were the ones walking past him, and he was a little surprised that in this fair climate should grow such thorny people as Frau Rupprechter.

Forty-five minutes later, he arrived back at his apartment, his legs sore, his head thrumming, and his rib aching.

He would've liked to take a shower, but with the bandage around his chest, no sooner did he turn the faucet on than he'd already given up. Just washed up a little, had a bite of breakfast, and by seven, he was sitting back in the crew room. Within moments, the alarm bell was going off, and somehow it all seemed perfectly normal to him.

And I don't know how the human brain functions here, either, if coming into contact with related elements actually does have an enhancing effect. Just like it's rumored time and again that boxers dope up with bull's blood and long distance runners with reindeer blood. Or if that, too, is just full-moon talk.

Two eighteen-year-old kamikaze racers with the vanity plates POLE I and ELVIS I had staged a duel in the middle of three lanes of commuter traffic on the stretch from West-bahnhof to Schlachthausgasse. The black Audi Quattro didn't come any closer to crossing the finish line than the red Alfa. Because first the Audi Quattro with the license plate Elvis I skidded out into the Gaudenzdorf median and then the red Alfa plowed full-speed into the Quattro.

Unbelievable, though! As Brenner was cleaning the brains of the two eighteen-year-olds off of the median, suddenly, something in his own brain stirred.

CHAPTER 13

Death might be big. But so is Vienna. If you take the 5 from Westbahnhof to Nordbahnhof, you'll be on the road for at least an hour. And you still won't be anywhere near the Bronx. Or anywhere near Grossfeld or out by the racetracks, or out in Schöpwerk, where they've got all the rapists and the gangs of youths and the newspaper people.

And you read in the newspapers how dangerous it is out in Schöpwerk, because of the crack, or whatever that junk's called that makes people so hot-blooded—makes them cut off your head. But nobody's writing about the deeper causes. Nobody's writing about the Burenwurst. Because eating a Burenwurst'll make you so aggressive, you won't hardly believe it. On the sausage spectrum, Käsekrainer, Zigeuner, Cabanossi, they'll all make you aggressive, too, but on a fundamental level, they won't make you anywhere near as aggressive as a hot Burenwurst, except, of course, for a hot Leberkäse.

When you're an EMT, it's not uncommon to end up with the stakeholders from a bar fight puking in the back of your ambulance. And you can be up to eighty-percent certain that you're going to end up with the contents of a sausage stand on your hands, mainly Burenwurst. I don't know if it's because of the grease or because of the circumstances. Maybe the sausage-makers mix in some kind of powder that stokes aggression.

I might've guessed it's from the mad cows over there. But cow meat, there isn't any of that in Burenwurst. No meat at all, actually. That's what Brenner's grandfather said anyway in his last years: Nowadays there's no meat in 'em anymore, only sawdust.

And so Brenner found himself reliving his old days because, as it turns out, his grandfather had been wrong. Because when they puked in his ambulance, well, it didn't smell like sawdust.

But here's what I'm really trying to get at. I was saying: death is big, and so is Vienna. And that's true, too. But it's a small world! Because Herr Oswald lived in Alt Erlaa, and so did Lungauer. And though it might be public housing, it's no Schöpwerk or Grossfeld, neither. On the contrary, high-class projects. Middle-class projects. Eight high-rise towers with as many occupants as all of Eisenstadt. With swimming pools on the roof and kindergarten and everything.

But Lungauer and Oswald sure didn't know each other from kindergarten. A of all, Alt Erlaa wasn't even built yet back then. B of all, Lungauer had been living here with his mother ever since the accident. And besides, he was only thirty-eight years old, so chronologically speaking, he never could've been in Herr Oswald's kindergarten class anyway.

Now, why do I keep saying "kindergarten"? Lungauer, a year and a half after his accident, was as helpless as a little kid. He sat there in his wheelchair, all sunken in on himself.

Brenner could tell right away that even sitting was too much for him.

He was as gaunt as one of those models in the photos that earn millions today. I always say, a woman can rest easy on a little bit of padding. But needless to say, for a fashion photographer, the film's the most expensive part. You've got to wind it and snip it and wind it and snip it, and come evening, you've used up a couple hundred meters of film already—costs a fortune. And so, needless to say, a scrawny model saves you a lot of film.

But fashion model's one thing—Lungauer's pitiful form was something else altogether. How he just seemed to be, I don't know, hanging there in his wheelchair, all skin and bones. And for that maybe we should be grateful that he did weigh so little, because otherwise he wouldn't have been able to hold himself up.

His greasy hair swabbed the collar of a brand-new jogging suit, and the way he just sat there like that, Brenner couldn't help but think of that famous universe scientist. I bought the book, too, and I have to admit, I didn't get very far, but still pretty interesting, what with the black holes and all.

Lungauer's mother showed Brenner to her son's room and introduced him. She spoke loud and clear like you would with somebody who's not all there—upstairs, I mean. "This is Herr Brenner! A new colleague of yours! From the Rapid Response Center!"

"Good day," Brenner said.

Interesting! Normally, Brenner never said "Good day." Always, always "Hello." He'd developed this habit back when he was fifteen or sixteen during a rebellious phase in Puntigam, and ever since, it's been "hello." And now, for the first time in thirty years, he says "Good day" all the sudden.

So you see just how far the rebellion had got with him. As if God had placed some kind of divining rod at the window, let the paraplegic dangle from it a little, gave a little wink: Look at you, already picking the "Good day" back up like some drunk bully picking up a Burenwurst, see here, you, too, could be a goddamned cripple.

Although you'd like to believe that, over the past few months of working as an EMT, Brenner had seen enough sickness and suffering that a sight like this couldn't shock him anymore. No such luck, though. As long as you're just the one driving and it's the other guy that's the cripple, it doesn't fully scare you. But when the poor dog's basically your own co-worker, of course, completely different situation. So "Good day" just sort of slipped out of Brenner. And I don't think any worse of him for it, either.

When Lungauer didn't respond, Brenner wasn't surprised. Because he didn't exactly look like somebody who could still talk—Brenner had to give Angelika a little credit on that one. His head was saddled to the side, leaning on his right shoulder, and a thin thread of saliva ran from the corner of his mouth. The one eye was kaput, while the other seemed to stare all the more for it. Despite the catheter bag hanging off the side of his wheelchair, you wouldn't have exactly got the idea that this was a top athlete submitting his doping-test sample.

But as Brenner turned back to Lungauer's mother, he

noticed Lungauer very slowly raise his right arm, centimeter by centimeter, and after an eternity, he stretched his hand out to Brenner.

"I wouldn't know," Lungauer managed to get out. It wasn't easy to understand. Brenner needed a few seconds before he was able to string the sounds together. But, then, needless to say: I wouldn't know!

Lungauer didn't actually speak all that unclearly. It's just that Brenner wasn't expecting the disabled man to bird-dog him like that. That somebody who hadn't seen a "Good day" in some time should make fun of a cowardly "Good day" from a healthy person.

It's pretty true, though: Only a person at his fighting weight could act like such a puny coward. Although in Brenner's defense, I have to say: Lungauer had the advantage of being disabled this whole time, whereas for Brenner, this was a whole new arena that he'd been tossed into.

"Herr Brenner is here because of Irmi!" his mother said, loud and clear again.

"Yeah, I know."

"You know what happened?" Brenner asked him, not as loud as Lungauer's mother, but still, louder than he normally talked.

Lungauer jerked his head back and forth on his shoulder because that was his way of nodding, and then he said: "From the lampshade."

"He heard it on TV," his mother whispered. "People think he's mentally handicapped," she said briskly under her breath, as though she were hoping: If I talk fast, he won't understand me.

"But the doctors say he's not. He's completely normal. He understands everything. Just like before the accident. Except the language center of the brain was damaged. The doctor showed it to me on an X-ray, where the screwdriver destroyed his language center. But it's not mental—it's got a name of its own."

"Aphasia," the disabled man mumbled from his wheelchair.

"You see, he understands everything," the mother sighed as if it were somehow unfair to her. "He understands it all even better than I do. Aphasia. Do you know what that is?"

"I drove an epileptic this one time. He had it, too," Brenner recalled. "He always called me 'crane-driver.' I think because cranes are yellow and our ambulances used to be yellow, too."

"He just mixes up words," his mother said, nodding along nervously. "But his thinking is completely normal. Just the words he mixes up."

Lungauer watched the two of them avidly as they exchanged pleasantries. His healthy eye traveled back and forth, always to the person who was speaking at that moment. It seemed to Brenner as if his healthy eye had doubled in size to make up for the other.

Back when Brenner was in the police academy, video games weren't around yet, but in the rec room, they already had an early precursor. And Lungauer's eye suddenly reminded him now of that game where you could play tennis with a white dot. For a few months there, he went up against Irrsiegler—practically every day they played Tennis for Two. When you hit the ball, it made this distinct sound. Irrsiegler went on to get in a motorcycle accident, and then, he auto-matically quit tennis.

When Brenner awoke from the hypnosis of Lungauer's eye, he asked him about Irmi.

"She was my coat."

"He means: his girlfriend," the mother translated, and Brenner came close to asking her to leave him alone with her son for a little while. "He probably said 'coat' because she always had that white lab coat on."

"Or because he had her love to keep him warm," Brenner said. "Or because she was just a buttoned-up kind of gal," he continued, and a little haughtily at that. "Or because she hid all his trouble spots. Or because with her on his arm, he felt like he could brave any conditions. Or because when he was a boy he had a camel-hair coat, and Irmi had fantastic humps."

"Hahahahahaha!" Paraplegic Lungauer nearly shud-dered right out of his wheelchair. His face was drooped downward the whole time, so it's impossible that he saw much of his mother's reaction out of the corner of his eye. He sure could've felt it, though, just how much Brenner's outburst had needled her.

Lungauer was beaming, incredible really, how his one eye could just beam like a beacon over his entire face. But all the sudden he gave an imperious stomp with his voice: "Room!"

"But while Herr Brenner's here, you have to keep us company."

"Brennerroom, too!"

"But Herr Brenner might still like to speak with me."

"With me he wants to talk."

"He wants to talk with you in his room," she translated, as though she thought Brenner was a little mentally handicapped, too.

I don't know why that was so uncomfortable for her. Not to mention the view from Lungauer's room—unreal, you wouldn't believe it. Only now did Brenner become fully aware of the fact that he was on the twenty-third floor. St. Stephen's Cathedral, the Ferris wheel, the Danube tower, the UNO building—all kilometers away, but you had the impression that you could reach out and touch them. On the far left, you could even see the towers of Vienna General. And one of those anti-aircraft towers that they put there during the War—the black behemoths just never got torn down. But the most conspicuous thing was that, in all of Vienna, there were practically no buildings left that didn't have those colorful splotches all over them.

"Hundertwasser must've tagged the whole damn city," Brenner said.

"Hahahahahaha!"

It gave Brenner a real kick in the ribs, the infectious laughter of this one-eyed Chuckle King. It's through peoples' laughter that you come to know them best. Because a cruel person can only put up a front for so long, but if you make him laugh, he laughs cruel. And a dumb person laughs dumb. And a prude laughs prudish. And a cynic cynically, and a complicated person, complicatedly—so you see, you can scroll through them all, but it'll always hold true.

Very rarely, though, do you hear someone who laughs quite like Lungauer. Pretty much the complete opposite of people with nothing to laugh about. Because they might be pretty and healthy and well-dressed and have a bunch of money and work in film or "media" or architecture. On the inside, though, they're so empty that the moment they open their mouths—immediate casualties. On account of the vacuum implosion. My two cents.

"At first I thought you might be working for Junior," Lungauer said, suddenly very serious.

"Well, that's true." Brenner was just playing dumb, though. Already he could tell that Lungauer wasn't trying to make a point just because he was on Junior's payroll.

"So you're a dog?"

"I sniff around, yeah." Because once you spend a little time with a word-twister like this one, you start to understand him better and better—it happens faster than you might think. And once you've been with him a little while longer, you even start to word-twist yourself. Brenner, though, no problems now: "Do you remember Lanz?"

"Angelika's father."

"He got arrested."

"I know."

"But his daughter thinks that he didn't do it."

"And he didn't."

"What?"

"Lanz didn't kill Big."

Was Brenner just imagining it, or did Lungauer suddenly get a little more fluent just now?

"I started at Rapid Response twelve years ago. We were three times as big as the Pro Meddlers were at the time. That was still under Senior. Then, out of nowhere, Pro Med grew so fast, they nearly caught up to us."

Every sentence took Lungauer forever. And even as bad as Brenner usually is about this kind of thing, I can tell you right here: Brenner's operating speed was exactly right for listening to a sick man tell his story in his own good time.

"After Senior died, Pro Med pulled the better political contacts. They picked up Watzek as a sponsor, and in return they got city contracts. We still had the better donors, though."

Brenner almost got dizzy, looking straight down twenty-three floors at the street below, as Lungauer continued talking.

"People don't know what to do with their money after they die—if they don't have kids, that is. Most of them leave everything to the church. Trying to secure their spot in heaven. Some of them appoint us as their beneficiary, though. That helped keep us ahead of Pro Med for a while. On the other hand, modern medicine. So, people are getting older and older and living longer. So we started getting fewer big donors. Because people just weren't dying."

I've always been vertigo-free, Brenner reflected. But the tremble that slowly entered his knees now had nothing to do with the twenty-third floor. No, listen up to what Lungauer had to tell him over the next half hour. It might've taken a healthy person only five minutes. But Brenner was glad it didn't go that fast. It was hard enough to digest as it was.

How Junior formed a trauma team with Lungauer and Bimbo. How Bimbo and Lungauer were always the ones to get dispatched where there were rich old ladies to be chauffeured. How they took a cue from Czerny, who'd coaxed a villa out of a widow. Unlike Czerny, though, not for their own personal gain, no, they did it all for Vienna Rapid Response.

"Unfortunately, that only worked some of the time, though," Lungauer stammered out. "So you court ten ladies, and maybe one of them gets the idea of leaving us something. And in spite of all of this, Pro Med still managed to expand faster and faster. Because needless to say, Pro Med had its own brand of widow care. So Junior starts to get suspicious that Pro Med is cutting in on his share of the elder-care market."

Brenner wondered why suddenly Lungauer wasn't mixing up his words anymore now. By his account, it was often just a matter of planting the idea in the old ladies' heads of leaving their fortunes to the Response Center. Because often they were so senile that they didn't know they even had fortunes anymore.

"So, Junior got a better idea. You know how much insurance paperwork there is, don't you, with the *Scheisshäusltouren*. So it became really quite simple to coax a signature out of an old woman without her even noticing that she'd just signed away her entire fortune to the Vienna Rapid Response."

"Could it be that you're only playing the part of the aphasic because you're afraid of what Junior would do if he found out?" Brenner asked rather abruptly.

"Hahahahahahaha!"

Then Lungauer was silent a moment. He took a breath so deep that Brenner got scared it might be his last. But then he carried on, as though Brenner hadn't said anything. "We weren't necessarily doing anything bad yet. Because if an old woman like that leaves her whole fortune to a bunch of hardhats or us, what's the difference? And the hardhats have got their own elder care, too. And so, all the sudden we had twice as many wills and testaments as before. So we were able to keep our lead over Pro Med for two more years. But then they inched back up on us again."

Brenner was still surprised that Lungauer wasn't mixing up his words anymore. Had he really been playing dumb this whole time? Or was it just the result of momentary concentration? Or did Brenner himself have a part in it—maybe he was unconsciously correcting for the mixed-up words?

I don't know. All I know is that as Lungauer went on, Brenner would've given anything for it to be a simple case of pathological word-twisting.

"The problem was that we were sawing off the branch we were sitting on. The better we worked, the fewer people died. The less often it was that we got left anything. But then suddenly three huge wills got executed in one month. Normally, three wills in a year would've been a lot. And the next month, four wills. Always on the calls that Bimbo and Junior took."

Maybe it's all just one big mix-up of words, Brenner thought, clutching at straws, as it were. And the saying's not for nothing when they say: you shouldn't clutch at straws.

Because when Lungauer said "died," he didn't mean "survived," but "died." When he said "euthanized," he meant "euthanized," not "resuscitated." And when he said "killed," he meant "killed" and not "saved."

"Then, three died in one thing," Lungauer said.

"Three in one thing?"

"Two in one day even. And the third later that same thing."

Week. Brenner wondered if there was a rule for when Lungauer mixed up his words and when he didn't. But you see, it's always the big questions that you send skipping down the longest pier because there's always something more important to inquire about.

"What was the cause of death?"

"Always the same thing," Lungauer said. Without batting an eye, he simply used the word "thing" for "thing." "You know as well as I do that one *Scheisshäusltour*'s just like the next."

Scheisshäusltour. I say, how sick can you be not to forget a word like that?

"Dialysis or diabetes," Brenner said.

"In this case it was diabetes," Lungauer answered. "The old ladies that Bimbo was supposed to bring to the hospital to get their sugar levels checked? Well, he'd just put them on a drip."

"That's what we do anyway with acute diabetic shock." Brenner didn't want to believe it at first.

"Sure. But Bimbo's drip was pure sugar water."

Brenner just whistled softly to himself. Not in the way that a person whistles when they've just heard something sensational, but that melody of his. You know the one.

But he was whistling so softly that it was inaudible, practically pantomime. The way a person whistles who's afraid of waking somebody up. A sleeping dog, say. Of course, it would've been better for him not to whistle near one such sleeping dog. Say, a bloodhound.

CHAPTER 14

And then, needless to say, out of the room. Out of the apartment. Out of the twenty-three-floor petit-bourgeois tower. Out of the whole complex. And into the taxi that Brenner had called from the Lungauers' phone.

While he racked his brain for who the automated voice of the taxi operator reminded him of, he was struck by a faded photograph next to the telephone. A young man exuding vitality, like a strapping farm boy from the old black-and-white movies.

"Is that your husband?" he asked Lungauer's mother, because the taxi operator still had him on hold.

"My son."

"Oh, you have two sons—"

For Christ's sake. Think before you speak, a time-worn rule. And Brenner would've been better off now, of course, if he'd observed his Latin teacher's old rule. Because, mid-sentence, two things shot through his head simultaneously: The automated operator voice reminded him somehow of his half-sister, who got married and moved to Berlin when he was twelve years old. To some guy named Gunter Schmitt. Brenner hadn't grown up with her, though, and in the thirty-five years since her wedding, he'd seen her at most two or three times, and believe it or not: sometimes he even forgot that he had a sister.

And needless to say, the man in the photograph was Lungauer himself. Before Bimbo bored a hole into his brain with a screwdriver.

He must've lost at least thirty kilos since the accident, Brenner guessed. Even though he knew by now that it hadn't been any accident.

Brenner kept his head ducked the whole taxi ride, because when you work in EMS, needless to say, the streets are just teeming with your peers who might catch you skipping school. After all, what he was doing was *verboten*—asking an 8K to take the wheel all by himself for an hour so that Brenner could do a little private investigating on the clock. That was at a quarter after ten, and now it was one-thirty already.

There was no real reason why it should've mattered to him now. Not after Lungauer had told him everything. How it'd gone from widow care to wills getting falsified. And then it went from wills getting falsified to wills being executed. And then, when it got to be too much for Lungauer, he took a screwdriver to the head.

And how Lungauer's girlfriend, then, continued investigating on her own. How Irmi had believed she could seek justice for Lungauer.

"Well, aren't we cheerful," the taxi driver said to his whistling passenger.

Brenner gave him no reply, though. It's always risky to give a Viennese taxi driver an answer. That's a cautionary nugget for you to take on your life's journey. Because, guaranteed, he'll give you an answer back, then, and generally speaking, not intended for your amusement. I'm not going to say anything else about it.

"Cheerful much?" the taxi driver asked again.

Brenner's answer was to quit whistling. Because it was only now that he noticed that perpetual melody back on his lips again.

He made it back to the station shortly before two. Slinked past the surveillance cameras in the courtyard and darted straight up to his apartment.

There he perched at his window, keeping watch over the driveway for Hansi Munz to return.

At twenty to three, the 740 pulled back in. Brenner ran down and intercepted Hansi Munz in the courtyard. "Do you have five minutes?"

"Sure."

"Can you come up to my apartment real quick?"

Though this surprised Hansi Munz, he nevertheless followed Brenner without any protest.

"Nice place you've got," he said, taking an appraising eye to the living room. "Where you'd get those nice walnut cabinets?"

"From my grandfather."

"Inherited? Not bad."

"Inherited. And he died all on his own."

"Dying tends to work that way."

"Yeah, most of the time."

"Death's the freebie."

It'll cost you your life, though, Brenner normally would've said now. And the last five thousand times he did say it. But this time: "Real funny."

"What's with you today? Did a louse run over your liver or something?"

Amazing, Brenner thought. How one and the same sentence can sound so different coming out of Klara's mouth than it does out of Hansi Munz's dumb mouth.

"Why'd you say 'liver'?" he shot back.

"Are you nuts? Why shouldn't I say it?"

"Do you still remember when Bimbo got that liver transplant? The day the Duke of Smoochester got shot?"

"Monday, May twenty-third, five-oh-three p.m."

"Why do you know the precise time?"

"It's not every day that you see a person get killed."

"Are you sure about that?"

"In the army, the smell of gun oil was enough to make me sick."

"And the liver transplant didn't make you sick?"

"What're you going on about the liver transplant for?"

"Can you remember where Bimbo was standing while he waited for his liver transplant?"

"Where else would he been standing? Right where we always stand, by Rosi."

"Was he standing there alone?"

"No, Lanz pulled up just ahead of us. That's why it took so long."

"Did you see Lanz standing there?"

"Why do you even want to know?"

"Did you see him?"

"You know damn well that from the parking spot you can only see the back of Rosi's stand."

"Did you see Lanz walk over there?"

"Hey, I really had better things to be looking at."

"You were watching the couple make out."

Hansi Munz tried on a filthy grin, but needless to say, a risky move. It's like when you're doing the high dive, and only when you're perched on the edge of the ten-meter platform do you realize that you chose a level that's too difficult, and then, when you don't quite land it, you look especially stupid.

His stupid grin erased itself immediately, though, when Brenner said: "And what if I told you that Lanz wasn't at Rosi's at all. Because Lanz was taking a donor kidney up to surgery."

"But then Bimbo would've been back at the vehicle with our liver transplants much sooner."

"Suppose he did something else in the meantime. You didn't see him, did you?"

"What's he supposed to have done, then?"

"Nothing crosses your mind?"

Hansi Munz didn't say anything. But the firmer he pressed his lips together, the farther his eyes popped out of his head.

"Well, aren't we cheerful," Brenner said, in the same tone of voice as the taxi driver. Which only made Munz look all the more alarmed.

"Are you nuts? Where would Bimbo have put the gun, then? They already scoured everything!"

"Did you drive the seven-forty today?"

"You know damn well that I've been driving the seven-forty ever since Bimbo died."

Munz was so proud of his retort that it quickly got the better of him. "Junior won't let anybody else behind the wheel of the new seven-forty. But next month, the new seven-ten's coming. By those standards, the seven-forty looks ancient. I'm telling you—it's even got an automatic transmission. If I get the seven-ten, you can have the seven-forty. Be sure to look into it when the time comes. All I can tell you is that those old crates we've been driving? No comparison."

Brenner was already on his way to the garage, though, and Hansi Munz was trailing behind because, needless to say, somehow he already had an uneasy feeling. But he never would've thought Brenner capable of this type of madness. Because Brenner walked right into the 740's garage and started tearing the vehicle apart. Hansi Munz began to hop from foot to foot nervously.

"Are you nuts or what? I've got to turn right back around and go out on a run! Don't you tear my vac mat out!"

But before he could finish saying "vac mat," the vacuum mattress was already lying on the ground.

And before Munz could shout: "And you don't need to go unfolding my body bag, either!" the body bag and the AIDS gloves and the gauze pads and the antiseptic wipes were already strewn across the garage floor.

And as Hansi Munz kept on shouting: "If you go and empty out my trauma kit, too, now—," the contents of all twenty-four compartments were scattered across the garage floor, and the transfusions, running into the drain. And the safety goggles and the butterfly bandages and the straitjacket and the crowbar and the oxygen tanks, all of it, dumped onto the garage floor by Brenner.

"I'm serious—you're going to be cleaning all this up tonight, I swear to you," Hansi Munz whimpered, as Brenner emptied out the towels and the first-aid tape and the burn dressings and the urine bottles.

Until finally, the garage and half the courtyard were so littered that you've got to admit, unbelievable what can fit inside an ambulance like that—more than in the garage itself, which, if you think about it, the ambulance fits inside of. In some ways, organization is just a good trick. But, flip side of the coin: the more immaculately organized, the more wildly the scraps fly when all hell breaks loose.

"Shit," Brenner said in a huff, after he'd emptied out every last thing and then saw what he'd done. "This looks worse than a clothes drive."

Because you probably know all about that, right? How the Rapid Responders are always holding used clothes drives, a great thing really. The fact that Bimbo was in charge of it, though, that you couldn't have known. And it only occurred to Brenner, too, when he said it just now.

And seconds later he was getting the key to the truck garages. And then, he was unlocking the truck garages. Three truck garages and not a single truck.

Because they were all crammed full of old clothes. You've got to stop and picture this for a second—and "old clothes" is misleading, because everything was high-fashion, brand spanking new! Everything washed and sorted, neat and tidy. Millions of purchases made out of frustration, you know like when your love life isn't completely ship-shape, and as a consolation, you go shopping and end up buying something that you wear all of once and then it's off to the clothes drive with that new wardrobe essential of yours. Three truck garages stuffed full up to the roof. Just let the meaning of the word "chaos" dissolve on your tongue. And think back to what I explained to you a couple minutes ago about my philosophy on organization.

"Don't you dare leave all that out in the courtyard, now, or else I'm taking you up to Steinhof and getting you locked up—you already pulled out the straitjacket. It'll only take a few seconds, Brenner, and then you're going to have that straitjacket on you. And Bimbo used to be able to get to Steinhof in eleven minutes. Eleven minutes, Brenner, until you're in a padded cell."

Hansi Munz got some backup now, too. Fat Nuttinger, in all his corpulence, was standing in the doorway to the dispatch center and yelling: "What's going on, Brenner? Don't you have anything to wear? You've got to ask first, though, if you want to take something from our clothes stash. Because they're for the needy Yugos, not for you."

Brenner didn't care about Hansi Munz or fat Nuttinger. And he wasn't going to clean up the clothes from the courtyard, either.

He just went back into the 740 garage, and there among the pigsty of his own making, he searched for the crowbar. The crowbar's intended use is actually for car accidents so that you can free the people who are trapped before they burn to death.

And not for the locker in the old clothes garage that only Bimbo had a key for.

Who knows where he hid it—maybe he gave the devil the key as a burial gift on his way to hell. Anyway, Brenner had no time for foraging now; he took the shortcut, i.e. crowbar.

That's when he saw the most beautiful breasts that he'd ever encountered in all his life. "Springtime in Provence," was the caption of the photo that Bimbo had hung in his locker with Steri-Strips. It must've been a pretty old photo, though. Because I always say, breasts as magnificent as those, you just don't find them anymore today. Whether it had something to do with the emancipation movement or not, I don't know.

Believe it or not: Brenner wasn't really giving the photo its due regard, though. Because underneath the photo was the screwdriver, and next to the screwdriver was a drill. But that wasn't any ordinary drill.

As Brenner walked out of the garage with the gun—which was so heavy that just carrying it nearly broke open his appendectomy scar—neither Hansi Munz nor fat Nuttinger made a sound.

All you could hear was a soft splash. From the rivulet winding its way to the garage drain from Hansi Munz's pant leg.

CHAPTER 15

"The decision is yours now: you can stand on the right side of history, or the wrong side," Brenner said, and I've never seen him this serious before.

"I always stand on the right side," fat Nuttinger answered.

"Then you'll go back to the dispatch center and look up a few things in the computer for me now."

"You think just because you've got a *Schweizerkracher* of a gun in your hand that I'm going to start dancing to your tune all the sudden?"

"This was Bimbo's *Schweizerkracher*."

"Bimbo?" fat Nuttinger asked, his brow furrowing. "Wait a minute, Bimbo who used to work for us?"

"Bimbo who shot Irmi."

When Nuttinger furrowed his brow like this, the skin-folds over his eyes resembled sausage links. "And all Stenzl did was throw himself heroically in between, like some kind of bodyguard, right?"

"All Stenzl had to do was hold his head up. But there was so little in that head of his that the bullet zipped right through like, pffft, nothing."

Fat Nuttinger just grinned.

"And if you let me onto your computer now"—Brenner just wouldn't relent—"then maybe later it'll look as if you took a stand and did the right thing."

But fat Nuttinger had no intention of letting Brenner into his dispatch system.

He was still enjoying the fact that Brenner was no longer under Junior's protection. Of course, he didn't understand that he himself wasn't under Junior's protection anymore, either. Because Junior needed all the protection he could get for himself now.

Little did fat Nuttinger know, of course, that a second later he'd be storming back into the dispatch center and barking into his microphone: "Seven-forty, return to station immediately!"

Because that was Brenner in the now-empty 740. He'd barreled out of the station so fast that the folks returning home with their shopping bags stopped to make the sign of the cross right there on the sidewalk. Although, making the sign of the cross doesn't actually have anything to do with the church of commerce. They've got their own rituals, you take money into your hand and then you give it to an officer solely responsible for such transactions, what's called a cashier. Making the sign of the cross, though, in and of itself, not really done. But when Brenner sped through the first red light with lights flashing and sirens blaring—forcing a tour bus to slam on the brakes—he saw a woman in the rearview mirror put her shopping bags down in order to make the sign of the cross.

"Seven-forty, return to station immediately!" fat Nuttinger barked again. By that point, though, Brenner was already long gone. And the shoppers, long gone, too—off to the first store they could find, and just as a precaution, purchasing something for the next clothes drive in order to keep the EMS, or the devil, at bay.

"Seven-forty, return to station immediately!"

Fat Nuttinger was a highly irritable person, but I can't recall him ever losing his dispatch demeanor like this before. Because now he was shouting:

"All emergency vehicles! All emergency vehicles! Stop Seven-forty!"

"Location?" the emergency vehicles radioed back.

"Unknown!" fat Nuttinger shouted.

"Six-ninety to dispatch!" Schimpl said excitedly.

"Go ahead, Six-ninety."

"Seven-forty has been ID'd on Triester Strasse outbound."

"Six-ninety copy. Follow Seven-forty!"

"Seven-forty is driving a hundred and sixty."

"On Triester Strasse?"

"Affirmative."

"Then drive one-seventy!"

"Roger wilco," Schimpl said, and with such grit, that I've got to say, theater of war's got nothing on him.

Then a brief hiatus, because fat Nuttinger had to dispatch a vehicle to a heart attack in the Herrengasse. But then, Schimpl, right back at it:

"Six-ninety to dispatch!"

"Go ahead, Six-ninety."

"Serious accident!"

"Where?"

"Triester Strasse, intersection of Anton-Baumgartner-Strasse."

"How many injured?"

"Three seriously injured."

"Attend to the injured at the scene. I'm sending immediate backup."

"Six-ninety to dispatch!" Schimpl wasn't even trying to keep calm anymore.

"Six-ninety?"

"We're the ones who are injured!"

"What the hell's that supposed to mean?"

"Vehicle overturned while pursuing the seven-forty."

"You goddamned assholes!" fat Nuttinger barked into the microphone, and then, unfortunately, Brenner couldn't hear how the rest played out because he was already at Alt Erlaa. He parked out in front of apartment block three and went up to the second floor, where Herr Oswald lived—at most a hundred meters from Lungauer.

Now, universal truth: men often make the mistake of not getting up when the doorbell rings at home. More often than not, it's the wife who ends up answering because the couch is just so comfortable, or Soccer Sunday, let's say.

And then, when the wife opens the door—too late. The unpleasant surprise is already there. Case in point: When Frau Oswald opened the door, Brenner saw Herr Oswald on the couch right away, and Herr Oswald saw Brenner in the doorway. But Herr Oswald thought he was seeing a ghost, and Brenner thought he was seeing an acute 21, i.e. heart attack triggered by seizure.

"A Herr Brenner is here for you," she said, turning to

her husband, and Brenner was immediately struck by her mannered way of speaking. A splendid look, I've got to say, hair all done up, full skirt and apron, the works. On TV she would've been the wife of a country doctor, but in real life she was just the wife of Herr Oswald.

And the furnishings, also quite elegant: white walls, white carpet, white leather sofa, white face on the gentleman of the house.

"Yes," he managed to get out, "Herr Brenner!"

"Long time no see, Herr Oswald."

"This is Herr Brenner," he stammered in his wife's direction. "We know each other."

"Do come in," she said to Brenner, friendly-like, and offered him her hand.

"No, allow me!" Herr Oswald intervened. "I'll see Herr Brenner out."

And then, needless to say, questioning look from Frau Oswald. There's this nice expression for when a couple of people are in a room and suddenly the conversation comes to a complete standstill. You say: An angel's passed through the room. I don't know where it comes from, either, maybe because in a situation like that you always get a creepy feeling, practically a draft from the great beyond. Almost like when you're shopping and you walk into a store and all the shelves are bare.

And while the angel was taking its sweet time strolling through this here room, Brenner remembered how yesterday he'd been leafing through an issue of *Bunte* in the geriatric ward. They had a photo of the fattest man in the world— he'd just died over in America—believe it or not: 420 kilos!

They had to knock out the walls just so they could get his corpse out of the house.

You're going to say, why didn't they just cut him up, would've been cheaper. But you see, a thing like this, it's a matter of tact. You've got to have enough respect for a person, I say, not to just go and carve him up for the sake of getting him out the door. Even if later on, you just end up burning him or burying him or portioning him out ten times for the lockers of an organ bank—it's a different thing than taking him apart purely for transport reasons. For once I've got to give the Americans credit.

What am I trying to say here. Brenner got the notion that the angel of that American behemoth was passing through the Oswalds' apartment right now at this very moment. That's how colossal the silence was that had suddenly engulfted the married couple.

And then Brenner said to Frau Oswald: "I'm from the EMS. And yesterday, your husband saved the life of a bicyclist."

These high-rises sway pretty easily, normally you don't feel it, certainly not down here on the second floor. But Brenner was convinced he could feel it now. On account of the boulder of relief that had fallen from Herr Oswald's heart.

"You didn't tell me," Frau Oswald said, and with a pride that gave her noble eyes a rather ignoble shimmer of emotion.

"He probably didn't want to alarm you," Brenner leapt in with an answer.

"But I would've been so proud! Why didn't you tell me, then?"

Dear women! If only you wouldn't drill so insistently

for secrets, then just maybe we men would dare creep out of our shells a little more. That would be my advice on this very fundamental problem. Although, in this case, of course, right out the window, because just one big house of lies anyway.

"The patient is now out of immediate danger," Brenner said, taking a swing at the next lie. "And he has no greater wish than to meet the man who rescued his life."

"Then you must go!" Frau Oswald exclaimed, and so resolutely that I have to say: a peeped-on woman would never talk that way to her voyeur. It's enough to almost make you understand Herr Oswald's inclinations a little.

She immediately fetched him his elegant jacket, and he put it on like a spineless child.

"See you later," his wife said, but he didn't say anything back. And as he took the elevator down with Brenner, he still didn't say anything, and as he got into the ambulance next to Brenner, he still didn't say anything, and five minutes later as Brenner raced along with lights and sirens, he still didn't say anything. And then he yelled:

"Are you completely twisted? Have you completely lost your mind? Are you insane? Are you a sadist? Do you want to destroy my marriage? Do you have any comprehension at all of, of, of—"

"Which question should I answer first?"

But the retort stayed lodged in Brenner's throat. Because meanwhile Herr Oswald had started shaking like an epileptic—such was the state of shock he was in that his wife had almost discovered his little hobby.

Needless to say, Brenner was sorry now that he'd disemboweled the 740 like a Christmas goose. Because otherwise all he would've had to do was reach into the trauma kit and give Herr Oswald one or two knockout drops. That would've calmed him right down, nice and fuzzy, to where he wouldn't be hysterical anymore but would still be capable of functioning. But Brenner must've been afraid that Herr Oswald wouldn't be able to cope with the task ahead in his condition.

Brenner couldn't come up with anything better to calm him down now than the cassette that Klara had slipped him when they'd said goodbye. As the first notes came out of the quadrophonic speakers, though, Brenner was already afraid it might've been a bad idea. Because music like this, powerful stuff.

Even though Klara's choir had performed without any amplification system at the time and without anything else, either, no electric guitars, nothing, just plain music, the likes of which you just can't find anymore today. Needless to say, this did nothing to get Herr Oswald to quit his crying. If anything, Brenner had to watch out that he didn't get started himself now. Because, memories and all.

He turned the volume down a little and told Oswald: "I know who shot Stenzl and the nurse."

Oswald, though, didn't react at all. Just kept on whimpering to himself.

"Everybody believed that Stenzl was the one who was wanted dead. And that Irmi just happened to be there—an innocent bystander, just an accident."

Oswald didn't want to know about any of this. He turned his back to Brenner—well, as far as the seat belt would allow—and stared out the passenger-side window.

"Come, sweeheet crohoss," the tenor sang. Klara had been right about that: "sweet cross," not "sweet death."

How, over the course of thirty years, had he managed to mix up those two words? Brenner was reminded of Lungauer with his aphasia now. The decisive word, though, needless to say, he'd got right. Because somewhere way in the back of his head, Brenner must've had sweet diabetic blood in his sights for some time now. Long before he knew that Bimbo, instead of rescuing his patients, was ushering them into the hereafter through diabetic shock.

But it was getting a little uncanny, even to himself now, as he thought back to when the melody had first started tormenting him. Because it wasn't just the day he met Klara again—that was the same day where the diabetic Frau Rupprechter had told him about how Irmi had been snooping through her papers, i.e. her will. The story didn't really register at the time. But way in the back of his head, it must've registered after all!

"But the truth is, it wasn't about Stenzl at all," Brenner went on. "Irmi was the target from the very start. And it was only to cover up his tracks that the shooter shot through Stenzl."

Brenner could see out of the corner of his eye that Oswald was torn. He was trying not to let anything show, but, because he was now listening, he'd quit his wailing, and by that, of course, he'd given himself away.

"I don't care," Oswald insisted, and looked demonstrably out the side window. But it's the demonstrables that give you away, of course.

"I told you about my co-worker, Bimbo."

No reaction. Exactly, though: too demonstrably non-reactive.

"The incident in the Kellerstüberl," Brenner said, digging a little deeper, "with him and the daughter of our other co-worker."

"You're the one who's a perv!" Herr Oswald said to the window.

"And that bothers you?"

"At least I'm not running to your wife and telling her."

"But your wife was downright proud of you."

"At the very last second," Herr Oswald whispered. And then he turned in his seat to Brenner and shouted at him: "At the last second! At the last possible second!"

Brenner was grateful for it, i.e. a cleansing storm to clear the air. Herr Oswald was gradually getting over the shock of his wife nearly finding out his secret.

"It all went over just fine," Brenner said, apologetic.

"Thank god."

And then, second attempt by Brenner: "But you do remember Bimbo?"

"Of course I remember! You think I'd forget a story like that?"

"Fair enough."

"Come, sweeheet crohoss," the car radio kept on begging.

And to tell you the truth: Johann Sebastian Bach knew exactly what he was doing, putting all that repetition into his songs. He knew what he could fairly expect from his lot, how you've always got to say things a thousand times before people finally get it.

Because it was only just now that Brenner got it himself.

Why he'd mixed up the lyrics to the song. Why, somewhere way in the back of his head, he'd mixed up the two words, just like Lungauer would: death and cross. Unbelievable, how long it took to make itself heard from the hinterlands of his mind: for the diabetic patients, the cross on the ambulances didn't mean salvation, but death.

"I told you how Bimbo was there when the two of them got killed with a single shot. And it's true, too: Bimbo was there. But not as a witness. Take a look in the glove compartment."

The *Schweizerkracher* was so big that it barely fit in the glove compartment. Oswald didn't dare touch it, just closed the glove compartment right back up again.

"It was Bimbo who shot Stenzl in the neck."

"Come, sweeheet crohoss," the tenor sang in an eternal loop.

"And who's responsible for Bimbo's murder?"

"That's exactly what I need you for."

Oswald gave Brenner an uneasy look and opened the glove compartment again. "Me?"

This time he stretched his hand out toward the gun but then drew it back at the last second.

"It's okay to touch it. It reeks so bad of disinfectant that I can guarantee you, Bimbo didn't leave a single fingerprint on it."

But when Oswald tried to take it out, it wouldn't budge a millimeter.

"Do you hear what he's singing there?" Brenner says.

"He's been singing the same damn thing for the last three minutes."

"Yeah, always just 'Come, sweet cross.' "

"His teeth'll rot before he gives up that old spoon."

It seemed to Brenner as if Herr Oswald was talking like an EMT all the sudden. Maybe it was the ambulance setting that was a little infectious, the adrenaline. Enough to make even a sensitive person like Herr Oswald grow some biceps—morally speaking, of course.

Oswald, though, right back to his old, insulting ways again: "What are you talking about a song for? I'd like to know once and for all what I'm doing here!"

"Bimbo treated diabetic patients with a glucose solution. Before administering it, though, he'd quickly hold up their wills for them to sign. He shot Irmi because she was on to him."

"You mean the EMS was killing people instead of saving them?"

"Come, sweeheet crohoss," the tenor sang seductively, as if it were the cross that men were always trying to get women to lie down on.

"Can you prove it?"

"That's exactly what I need you for."

Oswald looked dubious.

"You're going to have to hack into the Rapid Response computer for me somehow."

"I was afraid of something like that," Herr Oswald sighed.

"Number eighteen, is it?" Brenner asked, as they turned onto Novaragasse.

Oswald didn't even nod. And he didn't want to know how Brenner knew, either, that it was here where he kept his million-schilling setup.

How he financed it, well, you can imagine. But one thing I'll say in defense of his honor. His peeping fits were never on account of the money. And if he happened to extort a little on the side, never for his personal gain. All in service to the apparatus itself, every last Groschen honorably put toward the continual expansion of his personal surveillance system. And plenty of his own money he put into it, too!

The apartment itself can't have cost much. An outpost at best, without a bathroom or even a toilet. The computer, though, practically NASA.

While Herr Oswald booted up his machine and went to work hacking the Rapid Response computer, Brenner told him the rest.

"As their racket got more and more criminal, Lungauer wanted out. The day after he informed Junior of this, Bimbo and his screwdriver—"

"Seven-twenty, Brothers of Mercy!" Brenner was interrupted by Czerny's voice coming over the computer.

Once he got over his initial shock that Herr Oswald barely needed two minutes to tap the radio, he said: "You can make out the voices better here than in our own vehicles."

"I freely admit that I have better reception," Herr Oswald said, unimpressed. But then a good hour passed before he was able to verify all of the particulars from Lungauer's account.

"Affirmative," Herr Oswald said, after looking up whether on October 17 of the previous year, eighty-two-year-old diabetic Rosa Eigenherr did indeed die while en route.

"Affirmative," that Bimbo and Junior were in fact the drivers on this run, i.e. Big and R.I., because the computer didn't know their nicknames. Junior took the R.I. over from his father, but nobody ever got used to calling him that, only the computer bought it.

"Affirmative," Herr Oswald reported when three weeks later another diabetic died en route.

"Affirmative" that once again Junior and Bimbo had been the death cab's drivers.

"Affirmative," that on the twenty-sixth of November, a diabetic died on Bimbo's and Junior's watch.

"Affirmative," for Herr Haberl, too, the only man in the batch.

"Now we just need Frau Edelsbacher," Brenner read from his notes, "December tenth."

"How was that even supposed to have worked?" Herr Oswald asked, as he kept scrolling.

"Pure sugar water in the drip instead of—"

"Yeah, yeah, that's not what I mean. If Bimbo did in fact shoot Irmi, and only shot through Stenzl as a cover-up—"

"Or to throw Pro Med off track. Offense is the best defense. That's why Junior had me mucking things up over at Pro Med, too. Given their rivalry, no end to the dirt to be dug up there. And all just so nobody would get the idea of going after Junior."

"Granted. But how could Bimbo have possibly known that the two of them would be standing there making out at five sharp?"

"Do you know the fifty-percent theory?" Brenner asked. And then he told him about Klara's theory—and rather long-windedly, I might add—until he finally got to the explanation:

"Irmi had been prowling around all over the place, trying to see if she could find any record of Junior's illegal wheelings and dealings. That's why she went looking at the blood bank, too, because Junior was the one who'd installed Stenzl there in the first place."

"She made a fool of him," Herr Oswald said.

"Not exactly. That's where the fifty-percent theory comes into play. Because, in fact, it was the opposite. Irmi thought she was spying on Stenzl, but in reality, Stenzl was after her."

"Why's that?"

"Bimbo's orders. They'd known for a long time that Irmi was up to something."

"And for Stenzl to be standing there at five o'clock sharp with Irmi, Bimbo orchestrated that, too?"

Before Brenner could answer, though, Oswald said something else: "Alt Erlaa."

Because the whole time that Herr Oswald had been nimbly raiding Rapid Response's computer, the real-time dispatch system was up and running, too. And not just the radio, but all the frantic incoming calls, too.

And the whole time that fat Nuttinger's crack team of smug commandos were piping up over the radio, Brenner's aggravation was up and running, too. Nevertheless, he wouldn't have caught it if Herr Oswald hadn't said under his breath just now: "Alt Erlaa," practically, greetings from the home front. When all the sudden fat Nuttinger announced:

"Twenty-three, epileptic episode, Alt Erlaa."

"That's no good," Brenner said, instantly tuned in now. Because the address that fat Nuttinger had just given was Lungauer's.

And although he hadn't paid attention to the call at first—because the calls were running continuously—somehow he still had it in his ear. Somehow he still had the voice of Lungauer's mother in his head. With his one ear still reverberating, he distinctly heard Lungauer's mother calling for help.

Brenner must've had it stored somewhere, because somehow he was able to retrospectively retrieve it now.

But, you see, somehow just isn't enough. I'd love to let you believe that Brenner, in a supreme bout of concentration, managed to retrieve every word of Lungauer's mother, i.e. up with people, down with technology! But, in truth, it wasn't actually the call that Brenner was hearing reverberating in his head now—no, it was Herr Oswald playing the call back from the computer's memory:

"Come quickly!" Lungauer's mother cried into the phone. "My son's having a seizure."

Herr Oswald was sitting sovereign at his console like a captain on the high seas, mastering the most dangerous sound waves.

"It was one of your men, Nuttinger, who was here today, pumping him with questions! It got him so worked up that he went into seizure! Come quickly!"

Brenner was surprised that Lungauer's mother knew Nuttinger by name. But people out in the suburbs are often a little more casual, and anyway, her son did use to work with him.

"Now!" old lady Lungauer cried. "Please, hurry!"

"Come, sweet death," Brenner said for her. Because if it

weren't for Herr Oswald and his rig, her call would've meant certain death for her son.

And say what you will against technology, but without it, half an hour later, Lungauer would've been dead. And maybe people find it alarming sometimes that even the life-savers—the doctors and the hospitals and the ambulances— are equipped and armed to the gills, practically a private army. Practically, petit-fascism among the nurses, to use a high-caliber expression.

But that's just how it is wherever it's a matter of life and death. There's no place to be critical of society. So, once again, you find yourself reaching for the technology bomb, even if usually you'd say: Oh, the humanity.

And thanks to Herr Oswald's surveillance park, there was a gleam of hope for Lungauer now. Because they'd heard precisely how fat Nuttinger had informed Junior of Lungauer's mother's call. Of how Brenner had put the squeeze on Lungauer until he went into seizure. And only upon playback now did Brenner hear Junior over the radio: "Five-ninety headed out."

Brenner knew that the 590 still hadn't been fixed, that the tailpipe still routed exhaust directly into the passenger compartment.

"C'mon!" he yanked Oswald away from his computer. And within seconds they were swooping down the stairs like it was an acute 21.

"Junior's driving to Alt Erlaa right now to pick up Lungauer," Brenner explained on the way down. "Lungauer is the one and only witness. Up until now, Junior thought

Lungauer was too disabled to be able to testify. But now he knows that I was there. We've got to get to Lungauer before Junior does."

"We have to save him from the EMS," Herr Oswald said, still dumbfounded.

Brenner took the wheel. And I've got to hand it to him: If there really is a hell, then Bimbo was surely looking up at him proudly. Because from the second district out to Alt Erlaa, it's ten kilometers easily, and definitely, hold on, thirty, forty, maybe even fifty lights. And from the second district to Alt Erlaa, Brenner shot through all but one of them—you certainly won't catch me placing any bets over whether Bimbo ever managed that.

When Brenner rang the bell at Lungauer's mother's apartment, though, Junior had already been there and had already taken off with her son.

CHAPTER 16

Four hours before the Danube Isle Fest had got underway and the streets were deserted. Brenner had never experienced anything like it, practically a ghost town. When it came to red lights now, needless to say, he was at a bit of an advantage.

When the ambulance hit a rumble strip, the glove compartment sprang open and Herr Oswald reached for the *Schweizerkracher* again. And this time he actually took it out. But he wasn't prepared for it to be so heavy, and it instantly fell out of his hands and crashed to the floor.

"Watch it!" Brenner yelled at a lone pedestrian who'd just flipped him the bird for chasing him off the zebra stripes of the crosswalk.

"That's insanely heavy," Herr Oswald said, when he picked the gun back up.

"Yeah, it's not made of plastic. You can shoot two people at once with it."

"Not at once, but with one bullet, consecutively," Herr Oswald said, getting very precise all the sudden. "Where are we going exactly?"

"Paramedic Munz to five-ninety," Brenner whined into the microphone, imitating Hansi Munz's voice.

"Five-ninety. Location: Spinnerin am Kreuz," Junior responded instantly.

Then Brenner grinned as he heard the real Hansi Munz getting flustered on the radio: "Seven-seventy to all drivers! Who just said 'Paramedic Munz to five-ninety'?" Poor Hansi Munz, because he'd already suffered one humbling blow today by having to drive the old 770 since Brenner stole off in his 740, and now somebody's radioing in with his voice, too, and Junior's not even batting an eye.

"Seven-seventy, what do you want?" Junior snarled over the radio.

"Disregard, over," the real Hansi Munz said.

You and me, we know he was in the right. But it came off a little too sassy for Junior's taste. Of course, it was the unknown person imitating Munz's voice who was actually being sassy. But the receiver, of course, Junior. And not treating radio protocol with the utmost respect was, to Junior's mind, the absolute worst.

It didn't make a difference if you were driving a regular *Scheisshäusltour* or chauffeuring a person to their death, and it wasn't just about the radio protocol, per se. No, at its core, it was a question of aesthetics: either you present yourself on the radio as being in command or you don't.

"Seven-seventy, report, my office, tonight, over."

"Seven-seventy copy," Hansi Munz radioed, and Brenner imagined how the poor dog had just changed his pants and now he'd have to go trembling into the night with another pantload.

"Eight-ten, location: Franz Josef Hospital," a driver reported his location.

"Eight-ten, return to station," dispatch responded.

Transmissions like these, you hear them a couple hundred times a day, of course, in one ear and out the other.

Brenner, though, was becoming aware of the insistent way the driver kept calling in.

"Eight-ten, location: Franz Josef Hospital! Eight-ten, location: Franz Josef Hospital!"

"Eight-ten, return to station," fat Nuttinger answered for a second time, a little exasperated now, because some days a lack of discipline just seemed to infiltrate the whole radio system.

"Eight-ten, location: Franz Josef Hospital!"

Needless to say now.

"Eight-ten, copy," Brenner said. Even though, radio-wise, it really wasn't his business at all.

Brenner didn't mean it strictly radio-wise, though, because he had finally understood: 810 was Lil' Berti! And Franz Josef Hospital was only a couple hundred meters away from where Junior had just reported his location at Spinnerin am Kreuz.

Now, it's important not to confuse it with Franz Josef Station, where Brenner went to pick up the sandler a few weeks ago. Because the train station is on the complete opposite side of the city. It's just coincidence that they share a name. Then again, maybe not that much of a coincidence, because Franz Josef is a bit of a local Kaiser around Vienna, of course.

"Eight-ten: Matzleinsdorfer Platz," Berti reported.

"Eight-ten, I'm going to tell you one last time: return to station! And quit reporting your every turn to me!" fat Nuttinger said, fed up.

But now Brenner understood, of course, that Lil' Berti was following Junior for him.

Berti was on duty that day, and by this point, he must've heard the whole story about the *Schweizerkracher* and the 740, probably from Hansi Munz. And one thing you can't forget. It used to really get on Lil' Berti's nerves the way Brenner would imitate their co-workers' voices all day long. But now, of course, he'd been able to recognize right away that it wasn't Hansi Munz on the radio at all, but Brenner imitating Hansi Munz. And then, of course, he only had to put two and two together to guess that Brenner, for whatever reason, wanted to know Junior's exact location.

"Eight-ten: Gudrunstrasse!" Lil' Berti reported again.

Suddenly fat Nuttinger eased up now. "If any Rapid Responder sees eight-ten, tell him to return to station. Defective radio reception."

"Copy," Brenner, and ten other drivers, replied.

"Eight-ten: Gudrunstrasse."

Brenner laid off the radio now. He was afraid Junior might get an inkling that something was up.

And Lil' Berti laid off, too, or at least for a couple of minutes. Brenner could only surmise that Junior was still on the kilometer-long Gudrunstrasse and hadn't yet turned onto Laxenburger Strasse.

"Eight-ten to dispatch," Berti called in again.

"Eight-ten, can you hear me?" fat Nuttinger barked, as if he was thinking: If his radio's not working, then maybe he'll hear me outright.

"Reception crystal clear," Berti answered innocently.

"Location?" fat Nuttinger barked.

"Simmeringer Hauptstrasse."

Brenner couldn't believe how easily and completely Lil' Berti had fooled fat Nuttinger. How he'd managed to reveal Junior's new location as inconspicuously as possible.

"Return to station," fat Nuttinger said. But a second later, a new call came in—an emergency for Lil' Berti, as it turned out: "Eight-ten! Drive with light and sirens to Süd-Ost-Tangente. Severe fourteen! Critical Care Unit's on its way!"

Brenner swooped down Gudrunstrasse at breakneck speed. When Berti got diverted to Süd-Ost-Tangente, he was just two kilometers from Simmeringer Haupt, and as Brenner turned onto Simmeringer Haupt now, he could still see Berti in his rearview mirror.

And because he was still looking in his rearview mirror, Brenner nearly crashed into Junior in the 590. Because, needless to say, Brenner assumed that Junior would be driving full speed with lights and sirens. But instead, Junior was just chugging along the deserted Simmeringer Haupt, taking his sweet time. Which, needless to say, was a double threat now, i.e. speed of a funeral procession.

Brenner just said to Herr Oswald, "You stay put in the car."

"What are you going to do?"

But Herr Oswald could see the answer play out right there in front of him. And without any interference in between, like your average voyeur's accustomed to these days.

Because the windshield had shattered in such a way that the glass flew straight over their heads. When Brenner rammed the 590, propelling it through the window display at the Magic Moment Solarium. And the glass of the window display was sent spraying through the air like an explosion of sparklers, and for one brief moment, a spell was cast over the desolate Simmeringer Hauptstrasse.

Within seconds of the impact, Brenner was jumping out of his vehicle and tearing open the tailgate on the 590, where he was met by a thick curtain of exhaust.

"Are you all right?" he yelled at Lungauer, who was sitting there, sunken in on himself like he always was.

But Lungauer didn't answer. Brenner leaned over him and shook him, but Lungauer was very far away.

And the next moment saw Junior locking the tailgate from the outside. And then the vehicle started back up again. But not forward. And not backward. No, the vehicle slowly began to turn in a circle.

And the next moment saw Brenner throwing up. And the next moment Brenner knew that the next moment would find him unconscious.

Through the thick glass panel that separated the passenger compartment from the driver's cab, he could still see Junior shifting into reverse and trying to back out of the Magic Moment.

The sudden movement threw Brenner off balance, but he caught himself on the IV pole. But in catching himself, he broke the IV pole off its base. Brenner tried to thrash the glass partition with IV pole now. But something like this had never happened to Brenner before. Because today the IV pole was made of rubber! And his arms were rubber arms, too, today!

But the window wouldn't break no matter how hard

he thrashed, Brenner consoled himself, because it, too, was made of rubber today. And all the while, Brenner watched as Junior tried to back out of the Magic Moment once again.

A second later there was a crack so loud that in his stupor Brenner thought: Best Wishes from the Transmission. Even though he'd never heard a transmission crack like this before. It was as if, instead of an eardrum, Brenner had the whole window display in his ear, but his ear was too small to accommodate it, and the pressure suddenly shattered the glass into hundreds of thousands of minuscule pieces.

Doesn't matter how much you throttle the gears, a transmission just doesn't crack like that, Brenner thought. And maybe it's on account of the carbon monoxide poisoning that I heard the transmission crack as loud as I did. Maybe the carbon monoxide is just acutely sharpening my hearing right before it shatters my nerves into a hundred thousand pieces.

Or maybe Junior just drove straight into the 740. Maybe he didn't waste any time trying to back out. Maybe he just rammed the 740 onto its side like a snowplow. After all, if one car crashes into another car, that produces a powerful crash. Impossible, though, that it would shatter your eardrum.

Maybe nothing crashed, Brenner consoled himself: Neither the transmission, nor the 740, and the only crashing I'm hearing is my poisoned organs as I die.

Maybe the hereafter's located in a noisy part of town, and that's why my skull is buzzing like I've been strapped to the great bell of St. Stephen's Cathedral, the famous bell from the new year's eve show on TV.

You can't be mad at Brenner for getting a little hysterical in a situation like this. True, he should've known that Junior would lock him in. Nevertheless, whether he should've or not, if you were in Brenner's shoes, you wouldn't have kept calm exactly, either.

On the other hand, it can't be denied that the poison has its advantages, too, because he couldn't feel his broken rib at all anymore.

And about that bell, you know, the *Glocke* that always rings in the new year over here on TV, I have my own theory why that occurred to him now, listen up. His gun was a Glock, and as he marched alongside Lungauer now, taking long strides together toward the end of their lives, maybe out of some sense of solidarity, he started mixing up his words, too.

What I'm trying to say is this: he just wished he had his Glock on him. With his gun, he definitely would've been able to shoot right through the glass partition to the driver's cab. But alas. He'd taken his Glock out of the pocket of his uniform yesterday because it'd been pressing a blunt weight on his broken rib.

Driven to despair, and yet, a faint shimmer of hope for Brenner. Because the air seemed to be getting a little bit better now.

Maybe a little fresh air is getting in through the shattered windshield in the driver's cab, Brenner thought in his monoxide-rush. Maybe it was the crack of the windshield shattering that I heard. Maybe I'm just mixing up my words.

Maybe the thing that I call "skull" is what's raining

through the burst partition now and crashing against the rear door of the ambulance, causing the entire vehicle to re-verberate like that famous New Year's *Glocke*. And bloodying the whole interior with dark splatter—like in those turbo-orange-presses where you feed in ten blood oranges and a second later you've got a liter of blood orange juice.

Because the little slice of Junior's head that was still in-tact was truly like an orange peel that had been sucked dry and was now slowly sliding down the rear door. And his mustache, well, I'll only say this much: it looked as if some-one had tried to open a beer bottle with it.

And one thing to be said in all seriousness. For all the things that you could charge Junior with—embezzlement and murder, and strangling Bimbo in the end, too—he had more brains than those two kamikaze drivers from the Gaudenzdorfer Gürtel put together. One quick glance could've told you that.

Needless to say, though, Brenner couldn't see very much. First the poison had pressed his eyes shut, and then, the New Year's *Glocke* had flattened them into discs. And when he finally managed to squeeze them open slit-wide, an im-age appeared in that slit, which, compared to the brain on the rear door, almost seemed normal to him.

Because Herr Oswald was kneeling on the passenger seat on the other side of the now-partitionless partition. And holding Bimbo's *Schweizerkracher* with both hands. He was trembling so severely that Brenner was afraid the *Sch-weizerkracher* might accidentally go off a second time. And no wonder Herr Oswald was in shock. Because lightning like this only strikes once! All his life spent gazing, and then the first time he takes a shot, instant bull's eye—*auf wiedersehen* to Junior's skull and the partition in one fell swoop. I've got to say: Hats off!

And all the sudden, streaming faintly from the 740, Brenner could hear the tape that Klara had made for him thirty years ago in Puntigam:

> "O sacred head sore wounded
> defiled and put to scorn;
> O kingly head surrounded
> with mocking crown of thorn."

One thing you can't forget. The entire 590 was still resounding from the gunshot like one of those Asian gongs before the movies start. For Brenner, it wasn't like sitting in the movie theater, though—it was like he was sitting in the middle of the gong.

And street noise joined the Asian gong now, and the excited chatter of onlookers and honking from all directions, as though the Danube Isle Fest had the entire city of Vienna erupting all at once. It all blended together into an avalanche of sound, as if somebody had taken Brenner's eardrum and pulled it right down over his ears. And all the while, Klara's choir in the background:

> "What sorrow mars thy grandeur?
> Can death thy bloom deflower?
> O countenance whose splendor
> The hosts of heaven adore!"

Brenner looked Herr Oswald in the eye, and Herr Oswald looked Brenner in the eye, and the choir sang, and the drivers honked, and the curious onlookers encircled the vehicle, and a few nosy ones even stuck their heads in through the open passenger-side door and immediately reeled back around when they saw the *Schweizerkracher* swaying perilously in Herr Oswald's hands, and Herr Oswald didn't say anything, and Brenner didn't say anything, and Lungauer didn't say anything, and Junior wouldn't say anything ever again, and the choir sang:

> "Thy beauty, long-desirèd,
> hath vanished from our sight;
> thy power is all expirèd,
> and quenched the light of light.
> Ah me! for whom thou diest,
> hide not so far thy grace:
> show me, O Love most highest,
> the brightness of thy face."

Brenner heard only the distant choir. And just beyond the choir, he heard the police sirens which—I'd almost call it dotting the "i"—blended into this sublime experience of music now, too.

> "I pray thee, Jesus, own me,
> me, Shepherd good, for thine;
> who to thy fold hast won me,
> and fed with truth divine.

Me guilty, me refuse not,
incline thy face to me."

While the choir kept its distance, the police sirens got closer. And Brenner could almost feel the sirens overtaking the choir, closer and closer now. But not quite yet. The choir was still closer. The sirens had yet to overtake the choir.

And the chatter of the onlookers was closer than the choir. And Herr Oswald's hyperventilating was closer than the chatter. And Lungauer's snoring was closer than the hyperventilating. And the buzz of the Asian gong was closer than the snoring, and the deafening heartbeat—as if a drummer had set up his bass drum in Brenner's ear—was closer than the Asian gong. Though Brenner had never before experienced such sublime music, he prepared himself for the eventuality that it might be his last, this sublimely deafening experience, and he might never hear another thing for as long as he lived. But for this one second he was alive and could still hear:

"In thy most bitter passion
my heart to share doth cry,
with thee for my salvation
upon the cross to die."

And then Brenner didn't hear any more music. Just a bang that was a hundred times closer than the heart-drum in his ear. The choir, though, absolutely silent. Because with a single bullet, Herr Oswald had shot the whole choir dead.

"The only vehicle with quadrophonic sound," Brenner

yelled, because these days when your hearing's as poor as his now was, you automatically talk a little louder, "and you shot it to pieces!"

Herr Oswald didn't say anything. He just let the *Schweizerkracher* drop.

"Watch out!" Brenner shouted.

Herr Oswald didn't say anything.

"How are you?" Brenner cried over the din in his ears. Because he really would've been interested to know how a person feels when his whole life long he's known only watching, and then in an instant, he gets brutally thrust into doing.

But Herr Oswald didn't say anything and wouldn't open up, either.

"Good," a voice from behind Brenner answered instead. At first Brenner thought the brain on the tailgate was talking to him. Needless to say, though, it was just Lungauer, who—thanks to the shot that Herr Oswald silenced the quadrophonic sound system with—finally awoke.

"Good day," Lungauer said in his polite manner to Brenner.

"I wouldn't know," Brenner answered.

But today, Lungauer was too tired to laugh.

CHAPTER 17

Two days they detained Brenner at the police station until they believed his story. Maybe a little revenge was at play, too. Why they didn't let him go for so long. Because he was the one to solve the murder and not them. Practically, showed up his ex-colleagues a little.

And who knows how long the case would've dragged on without Junior's silver bracelet? But thank god they investigated the bracelet so thoroughly. Because on the inner band the word LOVE had been engraved, and it must've got sprayed with a little blood when Junior cinched Bimbo's gold chain around his neck in the 740 garage. Because in the engraved letters the police lab found a little dried Bimbo blood.

Saturday night and Brenner was back on the streets, a free man again.

He got on the U1 and rode it out to Danube Isle. Third day of the festival today, and in the newspapers he'd read that on the first two days alone there'd been over a million visitors to the island.

When he got off at the convention center, he only had to take a couple of steps before he was completely enveloped by the crowds. You've got to picture it for a second: usually you head to the isle because you're in need of some open air to move around in. During Isle Fest, though, all ten of its kilometers, like sardines in oil.

The event tents were only fifty meters apart, but you needed an hour to get from one to the next. And on the way there, you inevitably stepped on a Käsekrainer five times or slipped in mustard, every ten meters somebody spilling beer on your head, and it actually starts to feel strange if nobody's stepping on your toes.

Believe it or not, though, it suited Brenner just fine today. After two days in a cell at the police station, he actually had considerably more personal space there than he did here on the famous local isle, no comparison at all. Somehow, though, he just needed the proximity of people right now.

The biggest advantage was that he was unable to fall over. Because at the Danube Isle Fest, you've got people standing so close to you everywhere you turn that you automatically get propped up. On the other hand, it has its dangers, too. Because a drunk who's lost consciousness actually needs to fall over, just the body's natural defense mechanism, and that's why there are always so many deaths at the festival, on account of the unconscious people not falling over when they need to.

Brenner wasn't drunk, though. He was just tired from two sleepless days spent in an interrogation room. Not what you're thinking, though, torture. Although needless to say, certain methods that the Vienna police are a little notorious for. The old water-bucket method, for example. The Vienna police enjoy studying the critical reports on torture coming out of Latin America these days, and then trying it out for themselves. They don't mean anything bad by it—just some juvenile copycat mentality.

But with Brenner, you can rest assured, everything, by the book. Even a doctor for his broken rib. There was a completely different reason for why he didn't sleep, practically self-flagellation. Because he couldn't quit going back over the story, over and over again, from beginning to end.

How Junior had resorted to falsifying wills in order to stay number one in the EMS game. How he'd taken Lungauer out of commission when it got to be too much and Lungauer wanted out.

How Irmi had remained a problem for them, though. How Bimbo had instructed Stenzl, Junior's puppet at the blood bank, to keep Irmi occupied there a full five minutes. And how he'd shot right through Stenzl, ice-cold.

How Bimbo then became so cocky that Junior decided to clean up the whole case himself by giving Bimbo's chain a cinch. And how he'd tried to pit Brenner and Pro Med and the police all against each other so that none of them would come up with the idea of suspecting him.

I don't know, maybe it was the shock that kept Brenner in this state of chronic rehashing. Because when a head goes zipping past your nose, it's not exactly an everyday kind of thing. Or was it just some residual side effect of the carbon monoxide in the 590?

His hope had been that, penned in among a hundred thousand normal people, he'd start to feel like himself again here on Danube Isle. He trundled on, from one tent to the next. Concerts, skits, wherever he ended up, he'd watch, but he didn't fully take in any of it. Except for the hundreds of Rapid Response and Pro Med vehicles parked all over the place—on standby to go plowing through the throngs with their lights flashing. He didn't recognize any of his co-workers among the masses, though.

Around midnight, a Viennese rock singer went on, the closing act and headliner, and all the sudden Brenner realized who fat Nuttinger had reminded him of this whole time.

Brenner wasn't listening very closely, though. He just let himself get shoved aimlessly through the festivities by the crowds. Although I have to say, his feelings must've betrayed him a little. I mean, how aimless could he really have been? Or did Brenner's own will sway the throngs of people a little, too? Anyhow, suddenly he was standing right out in front of the Pro Med tent.

And then, he was standing eye to eye with Stenzl.

Stenzl stared at Brenner, and Brenner stared at Stenzl. From a distance of maybe two meters at most. But neither said a word. Not even a sign of recognition. And to this day I'm not sure if Stenzl saw Brenner or not. Because in a crowd like this, you could overlook your best friend standing two meters away from you.

And needless to say, Stenzl's best friend was not Brenner. Even if Brenner had in fact cleared up his brother's murder. Even if Stenzl had since learned that his suspicions about Brenner had been unfounded. But who likes being locked in his own basement for a whole day with three stooges from the cement works?

Even though it didn't do the Pro Med chief any harm; quite the contrary. It was looking like a sure thing that he'd finally be number one in emergency medical services now. With the triumphant air of an admiral, he stood amid a sea of drunks and stared at Brenner.

Brenner thought about what he could say to him.

A good thing you had me beat up by those Watzek workers, I could say, he thought.

Brenner still wasn't sure if the Pro Meddler even saw him.

If your men hadn't carried me back to the Response Center, then Junior wouldn't have put me on his three-week retribution plan, I could say. Then I wouldn't have met Klara. She was my high school girlfriend back in Puntigam who once made me a mix tape.

I'd rather not tell him that part, though, Brenner said to himself. He still wasn't sure if Stenzl saw him.

A good thing your guys beat me up because, otherwise, Lil' Berti wouldn't have ventured to find out who beat me up, I could say, Brenner thought. Then I wouldn't have gone looking for Berti at the Golden Heart. Then Angelika wouldn't have told me about Lungauer. And then we still wouldn't know to this day that it was Junior who was responsible for the deaths of your brother and Irmi and Bimbo.

That's how I'll start, Brenner decided.

But, at just that moment, Stenzl went off howling like a lunatic.

That was meant for a drunk who'd just puked on a Pro Med bumper, though. And then, Brenner was carried farther along by the throngs again, and he heard a little more of the musical stylings of fat Nuttinger.

After the concert, the crowds gradually dissipated, and Brenner lay down in the grass beside a litter of Coke bottles and beer cups and paper plates and dog shit and drunks.

He didn't wake up until early the next morning when the cleaning crews came through to clear all the crap off the island. He watched as the workers collected the trash and threw it into the orange garbage trucks. And he was surprised by how easily the street-sweepers scrubbed the asphalt pathways clean.

Inches from Brenner's nose, a trash collector pierced a Sunday *Kronenzeitung* with a metal nabber and stuffed it into a black trash bag. It was yesterday's edition; Brenner had already read it. The front page announced Rapid Response's new director, a retired city councilman and the former volunteer chief of the Vorarlberg chapter of the Rapid Response, so, basically a new beginning. And a polite person, too, who even visited Brenner while he was in custody.

Brenner stayed there in the grass for another half an hour, just watching the garbage trucks and the garbage men clean the island. They moved through the grassy fields, rousing the occasional drunks and sending them slowly on their ways, a moving sight somehow, almost like flamingos in an animal paradise.

The new Rapid Response chief proposed a mutually agreeable solution to Brenner's contract of employment, and Brenner signed on the spot. Three months' wages without having to work, not bad. And in three months' time, surely something would present itself. Besides, summer. If you're going to be unemployed, ideal timing really.

The new chief's only request was that he not return to his

apartment at the station. Because, crucial to morale among the EMTs that the grass grow as quickly as possible over the whole matter. The new chief promised that he'd arrange for the few personal effects of Brenner's to be moved and stored, all on Rapid Response's dime. And he even booked a room for him at the Hotel Adlon in the second district.

It was nine-thirty when Brenner checked in. Walked the whole way, a good ten kilometers. And along the way, a beer on Mexicoplatz. The hotel porter gave him an envelope containing 50,000 schillings. And sincere thanks from Lanz and Angelika.

You can't forget that while Lanz was in jail, he'd been rid of his entire gambling debt. Junior couldn't exactly demand the money back that he'd used to pay off Lanz's debt. So, Brenner pocketed the 50,000 schillings with a good conscience now.

He lay down on the hotel bed, but needless to say, huge disappointment. Because a musty hotel room, no comparison to the dewy grass back on Danube Isle. What he would've liked to do most was get right back up and take the train back out to the island. But he was just too tired, and besides, you can't make a nice experience happen twice anyway.

You can't make anything happen twice, Brenner said to himself. And I won't call Klara, not today, he said to himself. And not tomorrow, either. You shouldn't brood.

As he closed his eyes, he pictured the fleet of shiny orange garbage trucks and orange garbage men that had made all the festival detritus disappear as if by magic.

And this morning's experience of detritus and Friday's experience of music seemed to blend together into one and the same experience as he drifted off to sleep. And it occurred to him that perhaps it's only upon dying that a person has such a sublime experience of music. But he doubted that Junior, as his head flew smack into the rear door of the 590, had as sublime an experience as he did.

It's upon surviving that one has these sublime experiences, not upon dying, Brenner said to himself upon falling asleep. A good thought, he thought. Upon surviving, not dying. I mustn't forget this. When he woke up later that evening, though, he was just glad that he still knew his own name.

From the internationally bestselling mystery writer Wolf Haas

RESURRECTION

"Wolf Haas and Detective Brenner's debut shows how a washed-up private investigator can solve a double murder on a Swiss ski hill and become an Austrian policeman. If you like the Coen brothers, you will adore Inspector Brenner."
—*The Globe and Mail* (Toronto)

$14.95 U.S./Can.
Paperback: 978-1-61219-270-3 | Ebook: 978-1-61219-271-0

THE BONE MAN

"As Brenner chases the clues amid the picture-book countryside (one waits for a chorus of *Edelweiss*), he encounters sex workers, fake tour guides, war profiteers, slimy art dealers and even a white slaver. Fans of Carl Hiaasen ought to love this series." —*The Globe and Mail* (Toronto)

$14.95 U.S./Can.
Paperback: 978-1-61219-169-0 | Ebook: 978-1-61219-170-6

BRENNER AND GOD

"*Brenner and God* is a humdinger . . . a sockdollager of an action yarn, concerning the potentially fatal situation ex-cop Simon Brenner finds himself in when the two-year-old girl he's been chauffeuring is kidnapped." —*The Austin Chronicle*

$14.95 U.S./Can.
Paperback: 978-1-61219-113-3 | Ebook: 978-1-61219-114-0

ℳ MELVILLE INTERNATIONAL CRIME

Happy Birthday, Turk!
Jakob Arjouni
978-1-935554-20-2

More Beer
Jakob Arjouni
978-1-935554-43-1

One Man, One Murder
Jakob Arjouni
978-1-935554-54-7

Kismet
Jakob Arjouni
978-1-935554-23-3

Brother Kemal
Jakob Arjouni
978-1-61219-275-8

The Craigslist Murders
Brenda Cullerton
978-1-61219-019-8

Death and the Penguin
Andrey Kurkov
978-1-935554-55-4

Penguin Lost
Andrey Kurkov
978-1-935554-56-1

The Case of the General's Thumb
Andrey Kurkov
978-1-61219-060-0

Nairobi Heat
Mukoma wa Ngugi
978-1-935554-64-6

Black Star Nairobi
Mukoma wa Ngugi
978-1-61219-210-9

Cut Throat Dog
Joshua Sobol
978-1-935554-21-9

Brenner and God
Wolf Haas
978-1-61219-113-3

The Bone Man
Wolf Haas
978-1-61219-169-0

Resurrection
Wolf Haas
978-1-61219-270-3

Come, Sweet Death!
Wolf Haas
978-1-61219-339-7

Murder in Memoriam
Didier Daeninckx
978-1-61219-146-1

A Very Profitable War
Didier Daeninckx
978-1-61219-184-3

Nazis in the Metro
Didier Daeninckx
978-1-61219-296-3

He Died with His Eyes Open
Derek Raymond
978-1-935554-57-8

The Devil's Home on Leave
Derek Raymond
978-1-935554-58-5

How the Dead Live
Derek Raymond
978-1-935554-59-2

I Was Dora Suarez
Derek Raymond
978-1-935554-60-8

Dead Man Upright
Derek Raymond
978-1-61219-062-4

The Angst-Ridden Executive
Manuel Vázquez Montalbán
978-1-61219-038-9

Murder in the Central Committee
Manuel Vázquez Montalbán
978-1-61219-036-5

The Buenos Aires Quintet
Manuel Vázquez Montalbán
978-1-61219-034-1

Off Side
Manuel Vázquez Montalbán
978-1-61219-115-7

Southern Seas
Manuel Vázquez Montalbán
978-1-61219-117-1

Tattoo
Manuel Vázquez Montalbán
978-1-61219-208-6

Death in Breslau
Marek Krajewski
978-1-61219-164-5

The End of the World in Breslau
Marek Krajewski
978-1-61219-274-1

Phantoms of Breslau
Marek Krajewski
978-1-61219-272-7

The Minotaur's Head
Marek Krajewski
978-1-61219-342-7

The Accidental Pallbearer
Frank Lentricchia
978-1-61219-171-3

The Dog Killer of Utica
Frank Lentricchia
978-1-61219-337-3